About the Author

Jackie Dixon was born in 1949 in Dartford and grew up in Gravesend, Kent. She began employment, straight after leaving school, at the young age of 15 years in a local bakery in Gravesend, making trifles before venturing into London to work at IPC Magazines as a letter writer for Woman's Own Magazine. She later transferred to another department where she began training as a proof reader for Mills & Boone romance books. She also worked several years as an audio typist in various legal offices both in Gravesend and London. Thereafter she relocated overseas and worked in Saudi Arabia for many years until she retired and moved back to the UK.
Jackie Dixon currently resides in Sandwich, a charming small town in Kent, UK, along with her three cats.

Dedication

I would like to dedicate this book to my mother who was an angel on earth and also to my young great niece Jacqueline Carl who wants to be a writer when she grows up. I hope this will give her a little bit of inspiration.

Jackie R. Dixon

Gilroy the Fairy Collector

A CIP catalogue record for this title is available from the British Library.

ISBN 978 1 78455 407 1 (paperback)
ISBN 978 1 78455 409 5 (hardback)

www.austinmacauley.com

First Published (2015)
Austin Macauley Publishers Ltd.
25 Canada Square
Canary Wharf
London
E14 5LB

Printed and bound in Great Britain

Acknowledgments

I am grateful to the publishers for giving me the chance of finally having my work published. I am also thankful to my dear friend Irene who sat and laughed while reading my manuscript in its early stages which gave me encouragement to finish it.

Prologue

The secret village of Hemlock, hidden within the vast forest land of Inglescrubs, like most of the surrounding woodlands, had been a place of great delight and happiness until the areas had been threatened by Gilroy, the ugly Troll fairy collector, so ugly that the very bowels of hell would spit him up. His grisly face was a tangled mass of thickened scabby tissue with warts and ulcers that sometimes became inflamed, oozing and threatening to erupt. Amongst all the grisly bumps and lumps a great bulbous snout erupted in the middle of his face and huge hideous cauliflower ears with pointed tips sprouted from each side of his misshapen head.

His slightly bent grotesque but powerful stumpy body was also covered with warts and other unsightly pimples. As if that wasn't enough of protruding globular features, he also had an enormous stomach that bulged out as if a huge balloon was trapped inside.

He was a feast of hideous ugliness; not a pretty sight but even so, his endearing personality and quick wit was his only redeeming quality.

The tiny fairy sprites all lived in fear of Gilroy and many had fled their beloved woodland areas, taking solace in and around the hills and caves. Strange tales were reported and believed of Gilroy, also known as the Troll Warrior. Amongst others, it was said that he possessed a familiar, because he chanced to adopt a seemingly deformed, dishevelled Hog, who it was believed assisted him in his dastardly deeds.

Gilroy was renowned to roam around the woodlands with his faithful pet wild Hog, who Gilroy affectingly called Bogey; an equally repugnant looking beast, with a great snout and fangs protruding from its mouth. It was alleged that together they hunted and trapped fairies and gobbled them up.

Indeed there were numerous shocking grisly gruesome tales and a good deal of gossip about Gilroy; it was of general belief that he was known to be hideously cruel and relentless in his hunt for the fairies. Once he had caught the poor unsuspecting little creatures, he crammed them all in a cage which he carried at all times with him, strapped on his back. He prepared his daily fare boiled, baked, stewed or grilled depending on his mood. He was not fussy how old or young they were; they all went down the same way, very well done and crispy, fried or grilled in garlic butter.

For special occasions, it was believed, he liked to baste their small bodies in a spicy ginger beer fueled marinade and barbeque the fairies on a great open fire until their skins became a sticky but juicy crispy caramelized golden brown.

He would sit crunching his meal with enormous relish, frothy spittle running down his chin – fervent with desire and sodden with contentment. His grunting and slurping noises whilst enjoying his feast would send any other creatures nearby scuttling away for cover, lest the same be their fate.

According also to general belief, he was also not averse to capturing the very young trolls and it was said that he had even cooked and munched his way through all of his own family, cousins and all – he was believed to be a monster most foul and feared by many.

The Troll kingdom had expelled Gilroy long ago for his supposedly wicked crimes and he had been forced to live a lonely and isolated existence out in the wilds struggling to keep alive with the never ending black cloud of shame hanging over his head. He was just an ugly little Troll who nobody had wanted and he had taken to roaming around the dark hidden parts of the forest land often eating grubs and crickets to survive, which he later blamed for the poor condition of his complexion.

Because of his unfortunate appearance he was never able to make friends and as much as he had tried many times to approach the many different small creatures in the woodlands, they always ended up running away from him, horrified and repulsed by him.

There had been many a time when he had felt that his life was not worth living but then a little voice inside his head would tell him to never give up hope and he would feel suddenly renewed and full of optimism. Each new day became a challenge to him to do things that he had been afraid of the day before; his life became a never ending journey of adventure.

After all he had built his small cottage hidden in the thickest part of the forest land with his very own bare hands and had become totally self sufficient in his supposedly dishonourable existence. But although he had convinced himself of his own total independency and self sufficiency, he was nevertheless very aware of his own innate loneliness which he managed most of the time to repress.

The more obstacles that he had had to endure, the more it had spurred him on to face his fears. He had been determined to overcome all the obstacles of poverty and neglect and to leap over every stumbling block or barrier that had stood in his way holding up his progress in life. But now he felt important and powerful and no longer felt sad that he was an outcast. He actually enjoyed being hunted and feared and took great pleasure in having such a dark and sinister reputation as the cruel notorious Troll Warrior.

It was rumoured that he travelled far and wide to satisfy his evil appetite and lifetime habit of pillage and destruction, although he had been barred access to certain parts of the human woodlands and alerts had been put into action by Errol, the Sheriff of the woodlands who hunted him relentlessly day and night.

Nevertheless, Gilroy had over the years developed a most cunning mind, it had been a necessity for him in order for him to survive in his unfortunate circumstances, and, although he had almost been captured many times, he had escaped and gone into hiding in a great dark dank underground cave far below the forestland that he knew no other being would find or want to find, apart from the bats and the other gruesome inhabitants.

Chapter One

The evening was still and tranquil with a zillion sparkling stars gaily dancing and frolicking around in the vast blackness of the sky littering the heavens like glittering diamonds. The masterful moon hovered above like a grandiose bright lantern in the midst of all the splendid tiny points of light in the great ceiling of rich velvet darkness.

Although a chill prevailed in the air, the atmosphere was clear and dry as Gilroy and Bogey sat around their great crackling bonfire enjoying a belching competition after guzzling two gallons of ginger beer between them. Bogey as usual lost out to Gilroy, who far outshone him by belching for up to 20 seconds – he was enormously proud of his talented feat such as it was.

'You'll never beat me, give it up,' he said laughing smugly with a mischievous gleam in his eyes. A little green stringy leg hung out of the side of his mouth frantically flapping about, as he chewed noisily snorting at the same time.

'Some of us have it and some of us don't and unfortunately you do not have my extraordinary and unmatched talents,' he continued taunting Bogey.

'Hah, extraordinary and unmatched talents – I don't think so. More like unbelievable bad habits of an obnoxious goon,' Bogey scoffed.

'And, please do not speak with your mouth full – that is another obnoxious bad habit of yours,' Bogey said sniffing as a great green snot bubble formed from his snout which he slurped back in through his mouth with the speed of lightening.

'Oh gross – now who's an obnoxious goon; talk about a snotty nosed kid,' Gilroy said as he watched the green bubble vanish into Bogey's mouth. 'That is positively the most disgusting sight I have ever seen in my life.'

'Oh dear me have I offended your delicate senses,' Bogey replied. 'And by the way, burping is hardly classed as an extraordinary talent in any body's estimation.'

'You are just jealous my little repugnant friend,' Gilroy said.

'Don't make me laugh; I would never in a million years be jealous of a bag of wind like you.'

But burping was not the worst of Gilroy's odious noises. Great violent tumultuous outpouring of air could be heard erupting from his great behind – enough gas produced to create the energy of an atomic bomb, followed by a wafting of the most foul-smelling stench that could render any one nearby unconscious – the air around Gilroy gradually becoming polluted.

Gilroy had an unfortunate gut disorder at times and the symptoms, including bloating and swelling of his gut, caused him to pass tremendous blasts of gas and more often than not he had bouts of extreme and excessive discharging of the bowels. The only way of easing his discomfort was to violently let rip and disburse of the rush and flow of loose body waste – a positive great gushing and explosion of muddy murky muck.

His face would suddenly become purple and take on a multitude of distorted facial expressions of intense pain and torment. A lot of grunting would accompany all the straining, followed by a look of pure relief when the onslaught had subsided. The very process of this explosive condition would send his whole body into spasms of violent jolting and jerking motions on his privy, if he indeed ever made it in time to his privy, in which case the small hut would rock from side to side from the detonation of the bombs inside.

Bogey always knew beforehand when such a passing was about to erupt as Gilroy would touch his toes in order that he could raise and extend out his great behind as far as he could lo stretch his diaphragm to help release trapped gases and woe betide anybody who was close by, especially right behind him.

As a look of pure relief spread over his face after he just experienced one such episode, Bogey staggered before him gagging.

'Oh my God,' Bogey gasped frantically covering his nose and mouth with his large trotter. 'You should go and take a proper dump instead of letting rip on unsuspecting friends and neighbours. What you need is a state of the art toilet with super air-conditioning and an extra large grand bidet specially designed to fit your somewhat super larger than large backside.'

'I can't help it,' Gilroy replied stretching himself out. 'It's better out than in,' he said laughing. His raucous laughter sounded like a donkey being strung up by its hind legs.

'Yes, well next time warn me well ahead of time,' Bogey said wincing as he wiped off the foul smelling brown substance slowly dripping down his face.

Of course it especially didn't help Gilroy's condition that he adored ginger beer which he constantly guzzled with abandon; his fridge was always stocked full of ginger beer fit to burst.

The only other creatures remaining in the deserted areas were the hyenas who hung around scavenging for the tiny bones that Gilroy and Bogey spat out and tossed aside. They often fought amongst themselves for any leftover morsels of tiny bits of flesh and bone and their ferocious eerie snarling sounds could be heard from afar.

'Get orf out of it,' Bogey snarled at them. 'Thems are my bones and you can keep yer thieving claws off, otherwise I'll be ripping yer throat out with me bare teeth.'

'We are oh so tough, aren't we,' Ella, a female member of the Hyena pack, told him fluttering her long lashes. 'Come now, be generous and give a lady a 'lil bit of flesh and bone, will ya,' she said winking at him and pouting.

Ella was street wise and had been brought up rough and ready; she certainly knew how to deal with the low lives of the forest. Her one great advantage in her life was her beauteous appearance and enormous charm and this served her well and set her in good stead throughout her young life.

For a humble hyena, she was, and she was not at all modest about it, most certainly a bit of a beauty. But she was choosy who she would mate with and as yet had never come across another Hyena, whereby she could sit back and think – that is the one for me. Apart from that she just had no time to even contemplate looking after little stragglers running after her wanting attention all the time. It was as much as she could do to survive herself – so no little pups for her. And, after all, she was just a young pup herself.

'I'm just a kid myself,' she told herself. *I want to be pampered and see a bit of the good life before I am tied down in drudgery with a bunch of artful dodgers to take care of. I want to travel the world and have lots of beautiful clothes and jewelry and be wined and dined by rich influential men.* She had gone off into a world of her own almost forgetting Bogey standing in front of her.

'Aay up sunshine – good morning miss beautiful. How's about a 'lil kiss before I hand over the goods to you,' Bogey replied.

Without replying and with absolutely no hesitation Ella slapped him a little too hard about the back of his head.

'No chance of that and I'll take none of that boorish talk from you,' she told him looking more than a little irritated.

As always Bogey, in spite of her cruel and insensitive snide cutting remarks and insults, would give way to her and push some tit bits her way but if any of the other hyenas tried to get in on the act, he swiftly pushed them aside in the process.

Ella knew that Bogey had a soft spot for her but, *let's face it* she told herself, *he is no oil painting and if she did have his pups, by golly they would be a sight for sore eyes*. She closed her eyes tightly to block out such a hideous vision from her mind, visibly shuddering at the very thought of it.

'We could have beautiful children together,' Bogey said as if reading her mind, blowing her a kiss.

'Oh my God, just the thought of a bunch of ugly little wild hogs hanging onto my teats would send my entire body into spasms of alarming pain. Why I would be a sow with piglets and a swine for a husband – what a boar,' she tittered, yawning with hand over mouth. But on a more serious note she thought – *Oh God a sow can give birth to a litter of up to 12 piglets, about twice a year.*

'Just think what you are missing,' Bogey told her frantically rubbing the back of his head from the vicious blow he had received from her. I could bring you no end of happiness and contentment. We hogs are very social animals; we form close bonds and enjoy close contact – and we have periods of intense pleasure that lasts for 30 minutes – aay, aay – what about that then? I bet you don't get that with your Hyena boyfriends, do you? AND, we are very clean and toilet trained,' he told her proudly.

'Yes, I would feel about as much contentment as bathing in a pigging trough,' she replied.

'Right then, honky dory – Is that a yes then?' he asked her.

Chapter Two

The underground caves were believed to be occupied by the grisly vampire fairies, who it was believed, were thought to tolerate Gilroy for short periods of time only, as long as he brought a constant supply of captured blue fairies for their nourishment.

Popular folklore, amongst all the villagers around the woodlands and other small beings such as the elves, gnomes, pixies, imps, leprechauns and goblins, was that Drasilla, the majestic queen of the vampire fairies, was five hundred years old and had, also according to popular belief, a particular ferocious appetite especially for the small blue fairies. It was said that their blue blood was believed to give her extraordinary powers and to be particularly rejuvenating to her.

Mostly all such myths were passionately and persistently encouraged by the leprechauns, a roguish bunch of munchkins with puckish and deceptively light-hearted personalities. They had an ulterior motive as they truly believed that there were vast hidden crocks of treasures in the caves and they patiently waited for the day when the queen of the vampires would be forced to vacate the premises in order that they could be free and undisturbed to occupy the caves to carry out their search for the treasures.

As far as Drasilla was concerned, folk could believe what they wanted to believe and it frequently amused her how rumours continued to be grossly over embellished to such a degree. She always insisted that it was better to be immensely outrageous and ridiculous than ridiculously and immensely boring.

The legendary vampire fairies were said to be a mixture of fairies collected over time from different parts of the woodlands including the minuscule silver starlite fairies who created a shower of stardust whereever they went that fluttered down on the trees and ground. It was believed that this stardust was magical and created a protective haze around a creature or person in distress. These magical creatures could be heard singing in

Drasilla's caves, sounding like small angels in an enchanting choir, echoing throughout the caves in the evenings.

The Gothic fairies, also known as the Dryad fairies, had previously lived in parts of the woodlands hexed and tainted by black magic; they wore dresses made of gauzy cobwebs and had black lacy wings. It was said that this particular group of fairies were outstandingly adept at acrobatic ballet movements and were perfect for Drasilla's group of burlesque dancers.

The blue fairies were known to be the most beautiful of all with skin like silk, long shimmering blue black hair with exquisite violet eyes that glistened and all had long graceful limbs of perfect proportions.

It was said that the blue fairies had been especially selected and provided to her by an undisclosed but reliable source for the constant rejuvenation process that Drasilla had to undergo and that the skin and hair of the blue fairies were stripped from their bodies and transferred to Drasilla's body to enhance her beauty and give her eternal youth. It was also reported that endless vials of fresh blood extracted from the blue fairies were stored in a cold vault in the coldest part of the cave and that Drasilla drank two vials of this blood per day to give her special powers.

The fairies had all previously lived in the mushroom fields, quiet meadows and tangled hedgerows fluttering around carefree and joyously carrying out all their special tasks in the woodlands. They all waited patiently for the day to come when the woodlands would become free of the fairy collector and they could all return to their previous beloved realm.

Drasilla's girls, as she called them, were sectioned off according to their appearance. The very attractive blue fairies and Gothic fairies were immediately taken to the working entertainment class private section of the bordello where they were soaked, massaged, steamed and hennaed until they glowed ready for that part of her industry. They spent several months in training with the choreographer who taught them the art of exotic dance for the burlesque shows.

Other girls sectioned off according to their less than physical attractiveness were set outside to work as maids under the direct supervision of the Housekeeper and they were responsible for the cleanliness and good order of the entire dwelling inside and out. This was extremely hard work for them but they were happy and contented to be out of the woods and away from the danger of being captured by the evil Troll Warrior.

Each and every one of the fairies became a valuable asset to the thriving business of Drasilla's enterprise and she valued each and every one of them.

Drasilla was known to be a great beauty and it was believed, had herself been captured from the kingdom of the blue fairies hundreds of years ago by a wicked Sorceress, together with many sisters who now wandered ghoulishly around the great underground caves sometimes feeding on the small bats hanging around.

Drasilla particularly loved this tale and relished the description of having sisters wandering ghoulishly around the caves – at least it kept the undesirables out, apart from Gilroy.

When outside of the great underground, it was whispered that Drasilla and her sisters flew in groups and travelled vast distances to hunt and feed on small creatures of the woods who became victims of their macabre acts.

It was known that Drasilla's large workforce also included some stray members of staff, mostly humans from nearby villages that allegedly had been captured and taken to her caves and forced to perform tasks of hard labour.

But the truth was that Drasilla had a habit of plucking poor lost souls from the streets and giving them employment and a home in her magnificent opulent residence. Drasilla had taken on Mildred, one of the young women down on her luck from a nearby village for the position as her housekeeper. Mildred had full control of the way things were run overseeing banquets and formal dinner parties. Amongst other human members of staff also rescued from unfortunate circumstances were her cook Alice, a stout jolly middle-aged woman together with her husband Judd, the gardener and her handsome young Chauffeur, Mason and his loyal dog Wally, a massive but loveable scruffy Irish wolfhound.

Chapter Three

The legendary union between Gilroy and Drasilla had begun one such day when Gilroy had stumbled into the underground cave to escape Errol, the forest Sheriff who had been too close to capturing him. As he had slid further and further down into the darkness of the cave, he had found himself being ambushed by a large group of fairy vampire bats. He was completely overcome by the tiny group who between them had the strength of a great giant.

They had swiftly bound him in a thick ropy spider web so tight that he could hardly breathe. He looked around frantically for Bogey, his alleged faithful partner in crime, but he was nowhere to be seen.

'That is typical – he is never around when I need him,' Gilroy spluttered as he tried with all his force to break free from the tiny little squeaky rodents with their sharp teeth and tiny black wings fluttering loudly against his ears.

'I demand that you get orf of me immediately, you beady eyed little boggers,' he said through gritted teeth.

'Because if you don't, I'm warning you – you will regret that you set eyes on me,' he squawked.

He struggled to loosen the hold of the web and in his panic began to let out his notorious eruptions of foul smelling air from his behind, but much to his surprise, although they all began choking, it did not deter his captors from holding onto him securely. He could feel himself being dragged to a darker part of the underground cave and all he could see were a thousand little red eyes shining in the blackness. His fear heightened as he began to feel small jabs around his neck; he screamed out in pain as tiny sharp fangs sank into his neck and he heard suckling sounds.

'WAIT,' a shrill voice screamed out at all the tiny forms attached to his neck. The small pack of bloodsucking bats immediately disconnected themselves from his neck tumbling down around him, his fresh blood trickling down their small faces.

Drasilla, the queen of the vampire fairies, stood before them all, her magnificent voluptuous bosom heaving with anger.

'What is the meaning of this? You all know perfectly well that we have to test a victim before we can feast on it. You are all becoming careless and I will not tolerate sloppiness in my cave; I expect more from you all. I want pure untainted unadulterated nourishment – and, and this...' she hesitated for a moment. 'This diabolical murderous smelly Troll is not my idea of untainted nourishment.

'Go feed him to the sickly bats at the other end of the cave,' she continued. 'They will not be so fussy. And, please go quickly before I faint – My God, what is that awful stench; this grotesque great mass is absolutely filthy and stinking to high heaven.'

The small bats all dressed in pink tutus and tiny glittering tiaras were all looking at her with their mouths wide open wondering what on earth she was talking about. It was enough to be insulted by having to wear such costumes but to be ridiculed in such a way in front of this stranger was too much. She really did like to take a yarn much too far sometimes.

'Bbbbut, we are the sickly bats at the end of the cave,' the leader of the pack stuttered sheepishly.

'Be quiet, do not speak until I tell you to,' she demanded sharply pointing her forefinger at them ominously.

Drasilla ignored their expressions of sheer indignation as she stood waiting for Gilroy to speak whilst trying to stifle her amusement behind a huge diamond encrusted fan that she carried at all times.

Gilroy lay there mesmerized by her beauty; the sight of this beauteous woman standing before him filled him with delight and happiness.

'Oh dear lady, sweet meek maiden with your smiling ruby lips – turn not those smouldering eyes away from me scowling so tenderly,' he drooled, saliva dripping down his chin.

'Cut the crap,' she said with a smirk on her face. 'Is this man delirious? What have you done to him,' she then said turning to the small bats surrounding him.

'Don't let the sex kitten image fool you, there's Dracula underneath the mascara,' one of the small bats whispered into one of Gilroy's ears.

'The vision of your beauty dwells in my heart and though I may never be so blessed as to behold thee once more, that one withering look has stamped thee firmly in my heart like a dew-drop,' Gilroy continued visibly drooling as he crossed his toes praying to keep her mood sweet.

'Be quiet you ignoramus fool, if you utter one more sound, you will get much more than a withering look,' she replied, again trying to stifle her amusement.

'Look, errm your royal-ness, before you say another word and I do totally and unequivocally understand your disgust at my physical appearance but just give me a chance to explain myself,' Gilroy implored. 'I can be of great assistance to you. I know what you need and I can bring it to you your delicate-ness.'

He was after all desperate and could see no harm in begging for his life. He lay back gasping for air after uttering so many words in a row which had exhausted his strength. With an exaggerated sigh of anguish he laid his head back guardedly on the ground and resumed lying motionless as he stared up at Drasilla silently imploring for her mercy.

'And why would we need your assistance you simpering fool – you who are a vile creature hunting the poor unsuspecting innocents of the woods. You, who gobbled up your own flesh and blood; your own family, and then went on a murderous rampage around the surrounding villages and woodlands. No, no – absolutely not – I have absolutely no inclination, none whatsoever in no uncertain terms to go into any such alliance or even dalliance with such a vile creature such as yourself,' she ranted at him.

You are, let's face it, a wanted man – an outlaw in these parts. We certainly do not need your sort around here to attract attention to our, albeit infamous quarters – no one would be safe with you around. You don't actually possess any hint of moral discernment; you would never be able to understand the ability to perceive and be motivated by moral or ethical principles. Do you have any idea or have you ever had a feeling derived from senses or a feeling derived from multiple or subtle sense impressions.'

Drasilla's beautiful violet eyes flashed with intense anger in a cold, calculated and almost malevolent way as she herself stood there suddenly breathless after her ranting, her bosom heaving again.

'Oh dear, I seem to have exhausted myself,' she said breathlessly, one hand on her heaving bosom.

'It's OK, she often goes off on a tandem like this,' one of the bats again whispered in Gilroy's ear.

Gilroy continued staring up at her dumbfounded, his eyelids twitching, unable to comprehend half of what she was actually saying to him; all or most of the words were going through one ear and out of the other. He struggled to stay focused but could not help but splutter and stutter in answer to her barrage of insults to his senses.

'Whoa, wwhat do you mean, I mmmean, dddo I have any chance to spppeak here in defence of myself,' he blurted out stuttering and stammering.

'Oh for goodness sake, it's like trying to impart a sense of right and wrong to a child; I am trying my very best to instil some sort of self respect into your garbled brain; to impress ideas and principles to improve your current line of thinking, but I can see my words of wisdom are falling on deaf ears,' she continued sighing with exasperation, her eyes flashing with fury.

'I, I – can I just say this...,' he choked as he felt his throat closing and he was almost speechless with absolute astonishment at her words, hardly able to believe what he was hearing from the queen of the vampires – she who it was well known, herself hunted poor unsuspecting innocent creatures of the woods; she who had preyed on her own kind, and, continued to do so. *Well,* he thought to himself *there is just no arguing with women sometimes*.

'Look yer Maj,' he continued, 'What I am proposing is – that's if you could see it in yerself to just listen to me...'

'LISTEN TO YOU, LISTEN TO YOU,' she retorted loudly, finding it difficult to comprehend the nerve of this scumbag with his proposition. 'I wouldn't go into any type of agreement or enterprise with you if you were the last Troll on the earth. I can't afford such a scandal in my kingdom. Take him away now, I DON'T WANT TO LISTEN TO ANY MORE CLAPTRAP FROM THE LIKES OF YOU,' she shrieked at him.

'Now hold on luv – hold yer orses, will ya,' he said digging his heels in the ground as he was being dragged away. *It's amazing when a successful Troll is down on his luck – everybody kicks him when he is down*, he thought to himself.

'HELLOOOO – I said I don't want to listen to any more of your claptrap – I AM TELLING YOU THAT I WOULD NEVER, NEVER EVER, EVER NEVER DREAM OF GOING INTO ANY KIND OF DEAL WITH SUCH A DEPLORABLE, DESPICABLE MONSTOR SUCH AS YOURSELF. I don't believe you have the ability to make intelligent decisions or sound judgments and I fail to understand your morals; why you have the morals of a guttersnipe – you have a rough and vulgar manner. DO YOU UNDERSTAND ME,' she yelled at him.

'NOW WAIT A COTTEN FECKING MINUTE!' he screamed back in his defense and then remembering his unfortunate and vulnerable situation, quickly lowered his voice. 'First of all I am not sure what an ignoramus is or a guttersnipe and secondly, I know full well that I come from a lower class background and not from a privileged background such as yerself m'lady, but it's no need to make me feel like a total degenerate. OK, I'm all that you say I am; I am unrestrainedly and immorally self indulgent but I am not all that bad. All I am saying is that I can bring you a regular supply of blue fairies, as many as you need,' he stated emphatically, desperation dripping from his voice.

What am I saying, I'm talking utter and complete nonsense now, he thought as he cleared his throat noisily. He was after all humoring her, or maybe himself with this ridiculous pledge that he could not possibly adhere to, but he would think about that tomorrow. He also reminded himself that contrary to common speculation, the whole scenario woven around Drusilla's unsavory reputation was just a lot of hogwash anyway in his opinion.

'Oh, OK, done – say no more; that's a deal,' she said glancing at her diamond watch, which suddenly glittered brightly nearly blinding Gilroy for a few seconds. She had a very busy day and was not going to be hanging around with the likes of Gilroy wasting her precious time for one single moment more.

'Let's shake on that,' she said sighing, suddenly bored with the whole exchange as she stepped forward to his bulky frame and placed her small hand in his fat hand to shake on it. On touching his hand, she quickly pulled hers back with a disgusted look on her face when she felt a slimy coating on her hand.

'You won't regret this,' he told her, 'I am an honest trader and believe me, I take great pride in my integrity – Madam; you will not regret this – on my honor, I promise to serve you loyally.'

'Yes, yes, yes, I believe you – thousands wouldn't. Just save your nonsense for all your imbecilic friends – that's if you have any friends at all. Well, let's just say you've had a lucky escape today; I am feeling quite generous of heart today,' she replied grimacing, shuddering behind her fan after recoiling from his touch. It had been a most enjoyable little joke but now she was completely bored with him and felt sorry for the miserable little man.

She was after all also just humoring him; such a pledge between them was ridiculous but for now she would just let him believe that she was stupid enough to consider such nonsense.

'Now I have to go and wash my hands in carbolic soap – if you'll excuse me,' she added cringing, utter repulsion showing all over her face as she abruptly turned swishing her cloak behind her.

'Get over yerself,' he muttered under his breath as he watched her floating off back to her headquarters.

'Oh, and by the way,' she said turning back, 'I will have a guest room prepared for your short stay until it is safe for you to get back to your usual business, whatever that is – but in the meantime, we don't want any funny business from you, and I mean no sneaking around spying on us girls. Understand that this is just a temporary arrangement and I don't want you thinking that you can wheedle your way into my heart and home.'

'Thank you kindly Madam – I understand only too clearly and don't you worry your pretty little head about anything and I will certainly not be trying to wheedle my way into your lovely kind heart and you can be sure that I would definitely not dream of taking advantage of your gentle and compassionate self,' he quickly replied, averting his eyes from her, lest she turn him into stone.

'Yes, never mind about that, I still think you are just a dishonest despicable little slug of a thug and we will be watching your every move. And, don't even think about pilfering in my district – and if I so much as see you frying up any of my girls here, I will turn you to dust. I strive at all times to protect my kingdom and anyone who crosses me will pay with his life,' she warned him.

He mock saluted her as she continued floating onward. 'Yes, your drollness; anything you say your ghoulishness,' he muttered under his breath.

'As if I would want to spy on your skinny bones – I would sooner spy on a rat's arse,' he continued muttering to himself.

'I heard that you ungrateful hideous looking grotesque good for nothing Troll and if you are not careful I can change my mind about our little agreement here.'

Such as it is, she thought to herself. She was under no illusion that such a sorry looking creature could be of any use to her. But for now she would let it go and allow him to think that she had struck up such a deal with him. *I mean how anyone could survive with a face like that... and, as for that smell! Catch blue fairies, the very thought of it – why I would think that they would droop and die like little fragile flowers at the very first whiff of him,* she continued to ponder.

Nevertheless, it never failed to amuse her that the old story about her hypothetical appetite for blue fairies to maintain her youth appeared to be stuck like glue to her reputation, never to depart no matter what. After all she was just lucky to have such amazing genes and beauty that would never fade.

'Sorry, sorry me old flower,' he said mock bowing continually most ungraciously towards her but all the same chuckling under his breath.

'You are D E S P I C A B L E!' she screamed at him furiously, her eyes ablaze with anger, before flouncing off again.

'Despicable is good,' he answered mumbling under his breath.

'You are nothing but an untamed savage uncivilized and barbaric beast,' she continued screaming at him totally enraged now by his daring remarks in spite of his somewhat unstable situation.

'Oh my God, she does go on,' he muttered to himself.

'Bring me my smelling salts IMMEDIATELY,' Drasilla could be heard yelling as she disappeared through the dark long passageway of the cave.

She knew he was full of hot air and nothing very much else – but, she would find him something useful to do. Her business was very good and although she knew that it was based on an extremely sinister and dangerous theme, to say the least, it had proved to be a very interesting one and had surpassed her expectations of success by miles.

'After all,' she said quietly to herself, 'any good business must first start on a good interesting albeit sinister theme to get started.'

Chapter Four

As Gilroy shook off the now loosened ropy web that had been tightly woven around him and all the small bats had scurried off, Bogey suddenly appeared looking somewhat sheepish.

Gilroy groaned dramatically from the intense pain and torture that had just been inflicted on him. At every opportunity he always felt compelled to disproportionately exaggerate and magnify anything and everything beyond the limits of truth. Nevertheless, he felt excruciating jabs of pain in his head and the enormous mental anguish and agony he was suffering from was almost too much for him to endure, and, he was certainly going to make Bogey feel enormous guilt.

'Where 'ave you been while I've been tied up and near death's door,' Gilroy barked at him ferociously, flinching at the sound of his own voice as he spoke; the noise almost too much for him to bear – his head was positively pounding.

Bogey could see that he was furious beyond words and he was almost tempted to scuttle away with his tail between his legs like he used to do when he was younger and was being scolded in no uncertain terms by Gilroy.

'I, I was detained just outside the entrance by a lovely French speaking lady vampire Hog and I was terrified for me life – I thought she was going to suck me dry and gobble me up alive. Her name is Helena and I think I am smitten,' he answered gawkily, shuffling his feet.

'You what, I'll give you smitten, you swineherd you – you've made a right pig's ear out of me not being there to protect me,' he retorted, slapping Bogey across the back of his head nearly sending his head attire toppling off.

'Ouch, you're going to give me brain damage one of these days with your constant backhanders,' Bogey cried frantically rubbing the back of his head. No wonder I've always got a splitting headache.'

'Oh be quiet, you'll get more than a headache when I'm finished with you. And, what may I ask is that perched on your head?' Gilroy asked incredulously, but looking amused all the same.

'I's a beret what Helena gave me,' Bogey replied proudly holding his head high. 'I rather fancy myself as a descendent of the French renaissance.'

'I'll give you French renaissance – you never fail to amaze me with your daft ideas and ridiculous behavior. And get off my foot, will ya, yer great ugly clumsy lummox,' he barked as he turned marching off.

'Oh, don't be like that boss,' Bogey said ambling after him.

'Come on – let's get ourselves ensconced in the guest room that I was able to arrange for us while you were enjoying yourself all the time I was at death's door.'

'We're going to actually stay here with all these bloodsucking mutants – no Sir, not me; I'm off,' he said as he spun around ready to scuttle off in the opposite direction.

'Oh, with bloodsucking mutants he says, and yet, you were quite happy to loiter outside with femme fatal Helena,' Gilroy said snorting as he quickly caught hold of Bogey by the scruff of his neck before he had a chance to run off. 'Like it or not, we are going to rest here for a short while until the dust settles outside and the Sheriff gets tired of looking for us – for the time being anyway.'

Besides, I'm that tired and exhausted, I could sleep in a rat's arse,' he added yawning loudly and farting all the while as he ambled along the dark passageway.

'Pheweeee, I could say categorically that you are in fact a rat's arse; smell like one and look like one,' Bogey said as he quickly ambled on well ahead in front of Gilroy, before he felt another backhander.

'Less of the cheek – if I wasn't feeling so exhausted, I would give you a good hiding; you've let me down dismally today, I can tell you that. I'm that disappointed in you,' he continued still yawning and farting as he limped along. Sometimes he suffered with rheumatism in his old crooked legs.

'Are you OK boss,' Bogey said suddenly feeling guilty and full of sympathy as he stopped in front and waited for him to catch up. He knew that when Gilroy was in such pain, he limped quite badly and his legs creaked loudly as if they were wooden.

'So now you are full of sympathy for me, are you? Well, never mind all that. I just need to lay my old tired body down and sleep. I can hardly walk straight – there is just no rest for the wicked,' he said gritting his teeth.

Drasilla's expansive cave thereafter became Gilroy and Bogey's permanent place of refuge. As long as he supposedly kept to his bargain making regular deliveries of captured blue fairies in keeping with the deal with Drasilla, he was assured of a most safe and secret hideout when he needed it.

Well, that was the story that Gilroy initially chose to embellish and boast about. The truth was that Drasilla had engaged him as a Security Training Team Leader working with three Hobgoblins known as the Pug brothers as trainees and although he had been less than willing to partake in such a boring employ at first, Gilroy grew to adore his job. He especially loved the uniform he was given to wear and was seen to prance and strut around proudly bellowing out orders to other security men. He seemed born to lead and was given the respect that he deserved.

At last he had found his vocation in life; he had finally found steady employment that had previously eluded him all his life and he embraced his newfound career and new manner of life with enormous passion and gusto.

If only he could get rid of all his dreadful pimples life would be honky dory; he had tried all the miracle creams on the market but all had failed to clear his unsightly skin condition.

Gilroy had one objection to staying in the underground caves and that was the presence of other Trolls who were employed by Drasilla to guard the outside premises. Although he was a Troll himself, Gilroy particularly disliked the appearance of his race and felt that he was better and above the gruesome looking creatures; he was sure that he had been robbed of his true birthright and that he could not possibly come from such an ugly race of creatures.

The Trolls were an evil, crabby mischievous group of creatures, sometimes grotesquely disfigured, drifting in gangs throughout the woodlands and were at all times avoided and feared by the other inhabitants.

Ordinarily, Drasilla would have nothing to do with Trolls and although they often resembled the crafty and shrewd humanoid Goblins of the woodlands, the Trolls were by far the most foul and dangerous to deal with and that was why she thought they were perfect to guard her outside territory. She was aware of the notorious mischievous band of leprechauns who were intent on searching for hidden treasures in her caves but she knew that her premises were burglary proof with the most up-to-date CCTV Security Systems complete with new smart surveillance technology. She had a whole level in her cave with security staff on duty by the surveillance monitors.

Chapter Five

Gilroy stood parading in front of his mirror wearing nothing more than his grubby thermal underpants with a determined look on his face, fidgeting all the while, nervously hopping from one foot to the other and desperately trying to hold his bloated stomach in.

He was a very proud creature and accepted how he was, never feeling sorry for himself for his shortcomings in life and being born so hideous. He considered himself to be intelligent and above all good fun – nobody could say that he was not good company.

His only wish in his life was to find a good wife – a girl of his dreams who would worship him for who he was. His only problem was that he was far too fussy for his own good and always seemed to be searching for the perfect woman.

'Look yer majesty, I can't marry you – not now, not ever, not never – not a chance. I'm sorry... no, no; now listen I've told you so many times, I have to wait for the right woman and you are sadly lacking in certain qualities that I am looking for – I do like a bit more meat on my women; something to hold onto,' Gilroy said as he spat on his right hand and attempted to flatten a single strand of hair that stood to attention on the top of his head. No matter how many times he tried to flatten the strand of hair, it sprang right up again.

'Who are you talking to?' asked Bogey looking around puzzled as he walked into their quarters.'

'I'm just practising my speech to Drasilla when she asks me to marry her,' answered Gilroy as he stood facing his reflection in a big ornate freestanding mirror dressed in all his finery.

'Are you going soft in the head? Would Drasilla even think of asking you to marry her – I don't think so – not in a million years,' Bogey said sniggering.

'I'll have less of your cheek and sniggering at me disrespectfully like that. You will laugh on the other side of your face when I become the co-proprietor of this establishment – I will be the king and she will be my queen. I've seen the way she eyeballs me and checks me credentials out – she desperately wants to get into me breeches,' he replied still prancing around in front of the mirror.

'Why she is positively panting for me,' he continued puffing himself up like a huge bloated peacock.

Bogey stood there looking at him incredulously, his mouth wide open in utter astonishment.

'Hah, you wished – don't make me laugh, she is no more eyeballing you or wanting to get into your breeches than she is me. You're delusional, I tell you – you are kidding yourself, she is an intelligent woman; you've been hanging around here for too long – you're away with the fairies, so you are my fine delusional friend. Don't go spoiling things – she is a kind and giving lady but I suspect if you start acting in a nincompoopish manner, she will give you your marching orders in no uncertain terms – I'm telling you,' Bogey said wagging his hoof at him with conviction.

Just then Drasilla came floating into their quarters looking very uncomfortable and disconcerted.

'Listen you two and don't take this the wrong way but I've decided, or should I say I've arranged for you to be moved into one of the dungeons below where I think you will be more comfortable.'

Gilroy stood there scratching his head looking very perplexed.

'Don't look like that Gilroy. The truth is that I've had several complaints about a foul smell permeating from this end of my caves – it will just not do. I like to keep my cave sweet smelling and I'm afraid that is just not possible with you around on this upper level – so you will have to remove yourselves and transfer to the lower level.'

'What – but yer Majesty, the lower level is for the retards, zombies and the sickly bats and I feel that it is just not up to my standard of living in my important position as your main security training man. Besides there are no windows down there,' replied Gilroy as he turned to look at Bogey for some sign of positive opinion and support in the matter.

Drasilla stood there with hands on hips rolling her eyes. He really could be the most stubborn and irritating creature that she had ever met and at times he could be so tiresome that she was very near to telling him to pack his bags at times.

'What do you think Bogey?' asked Gilroy suddenly stepping back and inadvertently releasing a loud outburst of trumpeting from his great behind in his nervous demeanour.

'Ooh, begging yer pardon yer Majesty – phew just a little trump there,' he said hastily flapping one hand behind him in an attempt to fan out and distribute the foul smell into the air.

'Well Madam, as you can clearly see, windows would be very important for us,' Bogey said covering his nose.

'Oh my God,' said Drasilla, holding one hand over her nose and mouth. 'That is positively so disgusting – I'll come back; just get your things together and move down below as quickly as possible. You really have got to clean up your act Gilroy,' she continued quickly turning her head as she began gagging and choking, hastily making a quick exit from the dreadful stench wafting around the area.

'Now, see what you've done,' said Bogey. 'You'll have to do something about your gut – I've been telling you for years to get yourself sorted out, for goodness sake or I'm telling you, I'll be moving out myself.'

'Alright, alright, but I've told you so many times that I do not trust the doctors here – they are all a bunch of witches and wizards who don't know their arse from their elbow. Anyway, let's get our stuff together and move down to the level below. I can't believe that she would actually do that to me... unless, unless she wants to get me in a secluded part of the cave to have her wicked way with me. I've seen some of those dungeons and they are full of little gadgets; you know handcuffs and leather whips; I think she is a bit kinky – she definitely has her eye on me and wants to play some wayward little games with me.'

'Oh now you are seriously making me feel quite queasy and I feel like I am going to vomit,' Bogey said gagging as he spoke.

'Admit it now you are just so jealous because she favours me above all others, especially those ridiculously handsome dandies she allows to frequent the place,' Gilroy said still prancing around.

'Don't make me laugh – besides, if you haven't already noticed, those girls around here prefer to spend all their time with those young handsome rich dandies,' Bogey sneered at him.

'Ooh, you can be so hurtful when you want to be. But in a way that is exactly what I mean, she is tired of constantly being in the company of genteel boring men and is up for some rough now and I'm her man – I'm telling you, she has been planning this all along. Now come on, quick, let's get moving – I want to prepare myself.'

Bogey looked at him with amazement; he was strutting around like a nervous groom getting ready for his big wedding day.

'Huh, prepare yourself, my foot. I give up – there's no talking sense with you. You've been eating too much crackle and your brain's gone brittle.'

'Oh zip it, will ya; let me dream a little will ya; I don't ask for much and don't forget all my aftershave sprays and my antiperspirant – I'll need to smell my very best. Oh and don't forget my complexion creams,' he added as he stopped to stare intently into a nearby mirror scrutinizing his face. 'I do believe my complexion is starting to clear up nicely and just in time for my forthcoming wedding, don't you think Bogey?'

Bogey rolled his eyes in exasperation and with an exaggerated sigh and an expression of pure frustration; he stomped around collecting all their belongings, which were pitifully sparse and took him all of ten minutes to cram into their shoddy suitcase.

When they arrived at their new lodging area in the lower level, they found it more than pleasing – in fact they both stood with their mouths wide open in shock. Drasilla was a most generous and hospitable hostess; she had thought of everything they could possibly need; they each had their own bedchamber complete with their own en-suite bathrooms and their own separate phone.

Gilroy threw himself on the round bed adorned with a fleecy leopard skin throw, with excited gusto and complete lack of inhibition and self-restraint. With an exaggerated theatrical flick of his wrist, he leaned over, picked up the phone and immediately started talking into it.

'Oh my darling girl, my own dear flower – how are you this beautiful day; get yourself into your most alluring negligee and get your body down to my boudoir for some serious frolicking.'

'Oh here he goes – talking to himself again; completely delusional. Will you stop that; you are making a complete fool of yerself,' Bogey said, his eyes rolling again.

'Oh shuddup will ya – let a lonely old man enjoy himself for goodness sake,' Gilroy said as he slammed the receiver down dramatically, leapt up and ambled into the lounge.

'Oooh, we are such a delicate little flower, aren't we – have I hurt your feelings you silly old sod,' Bogey said tittering.

Walking then into the huge lounge, Gilroy looked adoringly at the glorious inglenook fireplace with its huge working fireplace where they could roast all manner of grand sumptuous dishes – a glorious buffet of gourmet skewers of sizzling fire-roasted meats to chew on.

Bogey could hardly believe his eyes as he looked around at all the refined furniture in the quarters prepared for them.

This must be a mistake or there must be a catch – I must be dreaming and I never want to awaken , he thought as he followed Gilroy around with his mouth wide open in shocked disbelief.

Gilroy rubbed his hands together gleefully as he walked around their new quarters. Everything was perfect for their comfort; they even had their very own chaise lounge where they could flop out in the evenings watching their favorite TV programs. A huge TV hung on one side of the wall which sent Bogey into ruptures of pure delight.

'Right, that's me all set,' he said excitedly, forgetting his initial reservations and feelings of misgivings and utter disbelief. 'I'm off to have a bubble bath and then I'm going to slump out on my very own velvet chaise lounge and just chill out for the rest of the evening watching some Turner Classic

Movies – I hope they have Sky here or Virgin – I'm not fussy.'

'Oh yea, and who is going to be cooking our evening meal all the while you are having your bubble bath and then after chilling out watching your old biddy movies, may I ask,' Gilroy said snorting at him.

'Enter,' Gilroy suddenly shouted on hearing a loud knocking on their door.

One of the ghoulish men servants appeared at the doorway. 'I'm here to serve you as you wish. My name is Claude and I am at your service at all times. Madam wishes to express her warm welcome to you in your new quarters and hopes that your new abode is to your liking,' he announced in a nasal whining voice as he extended out a tray with two Champagne glasses and a bottle of Dom Perignon Champagne and placed it on an ornate coffee table. After he had popped the cork off and poured the sparkling liquid into the glasses, he handed them each a glass.

Gilroy took his glass and immediately drank the whole contents straight down, finishing with an enormously loud belch. 'Oh that was wonderful – I'll 'ave another one flower if you don't mind,' he then said holding out the glass to Claude for a refill.

'Well, I was going to say 'cheers',' said Bogey as he sipped his Champagne gracefully trying to appear a little more cultured than his uncouth boss.

'Yea right – this place is a flea pit, not fit for man nor beast – OF COURSE it's to our liking you idiot; do you think we are blind – why it's so plush and luxurious, I could kiss you me old flower,' Gilroy gushed as Claude quickly backed away from him.

'Please do not do that Sir or I will be forced to practice one of my martial arts movements on you; my kick flick is lethal so you may want to forget about showing even the slightest hint of affection towards me if you value your child bearing years.'

'OK, everything is hunky dory then,' Gilroy said laughing, one eyebrow arched nervously as he ducked to avoid the spray of spittle. The man was positively worryingly gruesome beyond words.

Bogey stood there mesmerized by this man's huge Adam's apple, which was as big as a tennis ball and bobbed up and down as he spoke causing him to gulp continually and spray out frothy spittle. It also didn't help or improve his unfortunate manifestation that he had greenish teeth that jutted out giving him a distinct goofy look.

Claude had an extremely unbecoming sickly looking pallor – his face was drained, it was the pallor of mortal illness or of exhaustion close to death, but then being a zombie, he was practically walking dead.

Drasilla was known to keep a staff of male zombies specifically to do all the hard tasks around her enormous cave and underground quarters and, of course, it was heard that they were fed on nothing but bats and rats.

With his jet black hair slicked against his scalp with a centre parting and a bent over gait, Claude looked every bit a sinister character. As the main footman, he was the highest ranking indoor liveried servant and carried out many jobs around the cave – both indoors and outside. Drasilla generally selected her footmen based on good looks and a good physique which unfortunately Claude sadly lacked. His uniform for his general day to day duties was a coat with tails of satin and velvet, a starched shirt and knee breeches with silk stockings. As a rule Drasilla, again generally preferred her Footmen to have good legs, but, again unfortunately in Claude's case this was not one of his finer physical blessings; in fact he had no single physical blessing.

'Yes, of course, we are certainly deliriously happy in our new dwelling – that's for sure and we would be more than happy for you to prepare our lunch as soon as possible to start with.' Gilroy cooed as he then strode off into the direction of the kitchen and found what he was looking for. There stood against one side of the wall the largest fridge freezer he had ever seen. He hastily opened the door of the fridge section and to his joy could see rows and rows of neatly packed cans of Ginger beer. He then took a peek into the freezer and could see rows of little frozen bodies washed and ready to be grilled or barbequed in the great outdoors.

'And what would you like for your lunch?' asked Claude, gulping profusely as he spoke, again spraying frothy spittle in their direction as they quickly ducked.

'Oh one of those delectable frozen ducks packed neatly in the freezer and please be sure to prepare your very best orange sauce. I just love a succulent slow-roasted duck stuffed with orange segments and basted with a mouth-watering combination of honey, butter and orange juice, seasoned with Basil and fresh root ginger – positively DELICIOUS darling,' he gushed, saliva trickling down his chin.

'As I've heard, I thought your very favourite was duck with sticky honey and aromatic orange and figs,' Claude said sarcastically.

'Oh making little snide jokes are we? We certainly are in fine form today aren't we,' Gilroy said. 'I can tell you I certainly don't need any scathing remarks from the likes of you; I have to endure constant insults from my friend here,' he replied frowning, pointing to Bogey.

'Nooooo, please not figs today Claude,' Bogey quickly said. 'We don't want to repaint the walls so soon.

'See what I mean,' Gilroy said as he moved toward Bogey with one hand held out threateningly, ready to give him one of his notorious backhanders.

Chapter Six

Bogey had been abandoned by his mother a few weeks after he had been born in the darkest and dampest part of the vast forestland. His mother had been desperate and although she had not wanted to abandon a poor defenseless little newborn, she had had no choice in the circumstances; she had been after all weak and half starving to the point of total collapse herself. She had been able to feed Bogey initially but after a short time when she was too weak to help him any further, had managed to crawl away somewhere to hide where she could lie down peacefully and rest – she never came back.

When Gilroy had stumbled upon and nearly tripped over the tiny wretched little twisted form lying on the damp moss whimpering piteously, he had immediately taken pity on him and had scooped him up in his arms, huge tears rolling down his face as he looked upon the little wretched face.

Bogey had let out a little desperate cry for help and extended one tiny hoof out to stroke Gilroy's face, 'Dadda, dada,' he had croaked in his little baby voice and had inadvertently poked his tiny hoof up Gilroy's nose causing him to sneeze loudly. Of course Gilroy being Gilroy, farted uncontrollably as he stumbled from side to side trying to regain his balance while holding on to the little scrapper of a being.

In that single minute Gilroy's heart had lurched, threatening to jump out of his chest; he felt such love and compassion. He had wrapped the tiny creature in a tender embrace silently declaring never to leave it. This was his chance to have something that was his to care for and nurture with all his being; a little pup who would never ever leave him and who would love him without any questions or reservation.

Gilroy had broken down in tears at that moment, sobbing uncontrollably; here was a little forsaken rejected pitiful stray like himself and just as ugly to look at, well, not entirely as unsightly as himself but he was full of compassion all the same. He instinctively planted a wet slobbering kiss on the little face causing the little creature to cough, splutter and burp, hiccupping constantly.

When he had ambled back to his secret stone cottage hidden behind great gnarled trees in the deepest darkest part of the forestland where nobody would ever think of looking, he placed the little body down on his favorite armchair and began preparing some hot milk.

While waiting for the milk to boil, he stood picking his nose which he often did when he was deep in thought and decided there and then to call the little creature Bogey. *It was a good strong name with substance* he thought and suited the little lumpy face with the huge snout.

'My very own little Bogey,' he had whispered, feeling a huge lump rise up in his throat.

'I will always take care of you,' he had promised the little form, huge tears still rolling down his face like an avalanche.

Through the years Bogey never left his side and they did everything together. They could often be seen together marching through the forest with nets and baskets strapped on their back crammed full of crickets with their skinny spindly legs hanging out thrashing around.

Gilroy made sure that Bogey had everything that he never had himself. When Bogey was old enough to walk, Gilroy made him a bike out of scrap metal that he found from time to time. After all he had never owned a bike when he was small like all the other Troll children and it was something that he was determined to give to Bogey. In fact, Gilroy never had anything when he was growing up. He had been abandoned himself and never had any real family; he had been placed in an orphanage as soon as he had been well enough to leave the Troll children's hospital. Although the staff had treated him well enough, they were glad to see him go as he was an especially difficult child to care for, especially as he was forever messing his pants and the bed and then of course he had been banned for eternal time from the kingdom of the Trolls.

With Bogey he could be a better person and his life began to take on meaning for him because he had responsibilities and vowed to make a good life for himself and Bogey.

When Bogey grew older they became more and more like old friends; Bogey felt great love for Gilroy and would have done anything for him except sleep in the same bedroom. With Gilroy's unfortunate gut disorder, it was impossible to sleep peacefully breathing the same foul air without gagging the whole night.

Gilroy's only fear was losing Bogey eventually to a female hog who would come along sooner or later and sweep him off of his feet and Bogey would fall head over heels in love and leave Gilroy to live his life alone and forsaken again.

Bogey knew that Gilroy was fearful of losing him as he got older, but even if he did fall in love, he promised himself that he would never leave him – where he went Gilroy would go with him. Any female hog worth her weight would have to take them both.

Bogey had during his teenage years met a delectable young female Hog named Henrietta. Henrietta had adored Bogey and they had been inseparable but unfortunately she could not accept Gilroy being around, so she had to go eventually. Bogey had been broken hearted for months but the thought of having to leave Gilroy had been unbearable for him and having to make that choice between the two of them had not been easy for him.

Seeing Bogey so unhappy at that time had unsettled Gilroy and he had made a conscious decision to go look for Henrietta and beg her to reconsider the situation, but she had been adamant that it was her or him in Bogey's life – there was absolutely no room for the both of them.

She was such a pretty little Hog with bright blue eyes, long sooty black lashes and freckles all over her face. She had the most infectious giggle which had never failed to set off Gilroy giggling as well like a big school girl. It wasn't that she didn't like Gilroy but being around him, especially when she invited her friends over when with Bogey, was embarrassing for her as one by one they usually left when Gilroy released his trapped wind.

Gilroy had finally made up his mind to step back and early one dark cold morning, he packed a small back-pack bag and crept out of their small woodland cottage with a heavy heart.

Unfortunately, for him, that particular morning, he had very bad and excessive flatulence which made him wince as he attempted to move around as quietly as he could while Bogey was fast asleep in his small bedroom. As he stepped out of the door trying very hard not to make too much noise, he couldn't hold back any longer and he released his trapped wind – violent blasts of trumpet noises erupted and the expression on his face was of pure relief.

'And where do you think you are going,' Bogey had said as he suddenly appeared right behind him.

'Listen son, I've held you back all these years; all those friends you've lost because of me and now Henrietta. I want you to be happy and the only way for that to happen is for me to get out of your life and leave you to have your own family life with Henrietta and some little piglets later on running around.'

'Get your stinky behind right back inside before we both freeze to death. I don't know about you but I could do with a mug of good hot strong coffee followed by eggs and bacon. I'm going to get the fire started and we can sit down together and talk about this.'

'No look, who is yer Daddy here – I am and I don't want to hear you talking to me like that again – I am in control; do ya hear and this is something that needs to be done,' Gilroy told him as he drew his chest up in the hope of looking every bit a figure of authority.

'Yes, OK, I know who my Daddy is and as I said, get your stinky body back inside right now,' he had ordered him extending one hoof out towards the open door.

Gilroy had then rushed at Bogey with outstretched arms, wrapped his huge arms around his neck and had sobbed uncontrollably, huge tears rolling down his cheeks.

'Oh Bogey, I was feeling so miserable and didn't know what to do – the one thing I did not want to do is be selfish and hold you back from life. I don't think I would have lasted too long without you though, but at least I could give you a chance to get back together with Henrietta,' he had said between racking sobs.

'Quit your slobbering and blubbering – come on my old friend,' Bogey had said as he had guided him back inside. 'Sit yourself down and I will prepare a fire and make a good pot of strong coffee with a little something extra poured inside to warm the cockles of your heart.'

'Oh that sounds lovely me old flower,' Gilroy had said flopping down on an easy chair while Bogey pulled the bag from his back and threw it into one corner of the room.

'I'm that tired – I just feel exhausted.'

'You only just stepped outside the door for five minutes before I hauled you back inside – how can you be exhausted,' Bogey had said laughing. But he realized that life without his old friend Gilroy would have been dull and uneventful.

'And forget about Henrietta, she is far too young for me and she has already taken up with that other Hog boy who has been sniffing around her for ages when we were together – it didn't take her too long to forget about me,' Bogey had continued as he had begun spooning in some coffee into a pot and placing it on their iron cooker.

When the coffee was boiling and ready, he had poured out the steaming hot liquid into two big mugs and side by side they had sat together smiling at each other, tears of relief rolling down their faces.

'Don't ever do that again – I would be lost without you and I don't think I would ever get used to the fresh air around here when you were gone,' Bogey had told him laughing and crying at the same time.

'Oh, you say the nicest things to me,' Gilroy had said in between gulping his coffee down and torrential tears flooding down his face like an overflowing river, but this time the tears were tears of happiness and relief.

Chapter Seven

Drasilla concluded her daily inspection tour of her cave and was as usual pleased with how her business was running smoothly. She was very impressed with the way Gilroy was taking his position seriously. In spite of his motley appearance he had definite charisma and most people seemed to just trust him the longer they got to know him. She supposed it had something to do with that inner kindness and compassion that he seemed to possess inside; it was something that she had recognized when she had first met him.

In a lot of ways they were both very similar, apart from obvious dissimilarities. In her own way, she had built up a family by drawing in people she knew she could trust and she felt that Gilroy was exactly the same type.

She had decided to promote him to Chief of her Security Unit and her board of Directors had cast a vote in favor although one particular member had opposed the vote quite passionately and this had worried her.

Dargo, half man and half eagle was Drasilla's personal body guard and he guarded her fiercely as a mother wolf would guard her cubs. He had passionately opposed the vote to promote Gilroy as he did not trust Gilroy and considered him to be a most foul, miserable and filthy creature not fit to even be in the vicinity of Drasilla's dwelling.

Drasilla knew that it had everything to do with the disappearance of his family and he had never trusted any of the Trolls since his wife and daughter had been taken from him. It was well known that it was the Troll Warrior who had kidnapped his wife and daughter.

Nevertheless, Drasilla had gone ahead with her decision for the promotion and planned to inform Gilroy later – she knew he would be delighted by the good news.

Just then her intercom rang and she picked it up immediately; her receptionist Cora informed her that the Chief of Police was on the line wishing to speak to her with some urgency.

Cora, a Gothic fairy, was a loyal member of Drasilla's staff and had been working with her as a receptionist/telephonist for the most part of five hundred years. It was for this reason that Drasilla put up with a most unfortunate habit that she had picked up over the years; she had become a chain smoker causing her to continually splutter and cough – it was a most unattractive sight. This aggravated Drasilla no end but she had trained herself to grit her teeth when listening to her.

'The Sheriff is on the line,' Cora now informed her, coughing and spluttering.

'Oh, for goodness sake,' said Gertie, Cora's twin sister, seated next to her. 'Thank you very much – you have now coated my cheese and pickle sandwich with cigarette ash.'

'Now, now girls let's not fight. OK Cora go ahead and put him through and please take that cigarette out of the corner of your mouth when speaking on the phone in future – it is most unattractive and so bad for your skin,' Drasilla said sighing, while she lit up one of her peppermint cigarettes. Peppermint Herbal Cigarettes had been an enormous help to her during the period of withdrawal when she wanted to quit smoking hard tobacco cigarettes. She had been unable to her curb her urge for a tobacco smoke until she discovered Peppermint Herbal Cigarettes recommended to her by the local Wizard/village herbalist Gruntle and with his help she had gradually been able to reduce her habit, unlike Cora.

Cora and Gertie were like daughters to her and in spite of the fact that they constantly bickered together, they were ordinarily, apart from being sisters, the best of friends and she valued them both in her business. They were both very smart and attractive in appearance and fronted her business perfectly as receptionists.

She heard the line click as Cora connected her with Errol, the village Sheriff.

'Well hello there my darling and what can I do for you. Long time, no see! I am very disappointed with you my darling; you have not visited me and my girls for some time now. So, what is it my darling Errol? Are my girls no longer exciting for you now that you have become a respectable married man.'

'Now, please do not talk to me like that Drasilla – you know I am a very respectable member of the community now – not that I wasn't before. I am still the County Sheriff and you know why I can't visit your premises now.'

'Yes, I can imagine, and talk about rubbing salt into my wound; you go and marry Labelle – my arch-enemy, no less. I am so hurt that you would even prefer that insipid looking Gothic bat and I can't imagine why her uninspiring designs are so popular,' she replied sarcastically.

'Well, you should know Drasilla – you order them by the dozen and most of her success these days is largely due to your regular orders.'

All female members of the cave wore similar outfits in keeping with the way Drasilla liked to be represented. Unlike her own attire, all the females wore black brocade Goth tail coat jackets with burlesque pink bustle tutu mini-skirts and quality black seamed stockings with burlesque garters.

'Yes, well, my clientele are quite enamored by my girl's attire – all thanks to Labelle, I suppose,' she said unenthusiastically, her eyes rolling.

'And, not to mention, you yourself wear her designs all the time now and I am told by Labelle that you absolutely love all of her floating style gowns – so you can't say that her particular style of fashion is uninspiring,' Errol replied smugly.

'OK, OK, I get the point – now what can I do for you today Errol, my darling,' Drasilla replied sighing impatiently.

'Well, I have to tell you Drasilla that your bordello business and burlesque shows have become quite the talk of the villages and the majority of village folk want to have your establishment closed down especially the leprechauns on the basis that you are conducting an illegal business enterprise. Now I am not saying that I agree with them and I have placated most of them, except the leprechauns and hopefully things will settle down eventually. My urgent concern though is that I have been hearing rumors that you have been harboring a wanted man, a dangerous criminal in your premises – this is a serious offense Drasilla and you could be looking at a harsh sentence, not to mention your ill-gotten gains as a Madam running a bordello. If these rumors are true, you must turn this person in immediately and I will try to protect you. If however you have absolutely no idea that he is in fact hiding in your premises – if you know what I am trying to say, I'm sure we could be lenient with you.'

'Oh, and yes my darling – let's not forget your regular contributions to my ill-gotten gains,' she quickly replied feeling a little miffed at that moment by his careless remarks. She was determined to deliberately avoid the actual issue that he was making reference to.

'Now don't go off the subject like that Drasilla and you know fine full well that my regular contributions as you call them no longer exist – I no longer visit your premises for light entertainment. But anyway, I will have to pay a visit to your premises again – an official visit you understand, to question you about harboring the said fugitive.'

'And, who may this fugitive be, may I ask darling?' she replied dripping sarcasm.

'As if you didn't know – you know fine full well whom I am referring to,' Errol said sighing with irritation.

'Gilroy, the Troll Warrior or the fairy collector, as he is frequently called, has been known to frequent your premises and I have it on good authority that he has been a guest on many occasions due to a business deal set up between you and he,' he continued.

'Well, I can categorically promise you that Gilroy is not a frequent visitor to my premises; my girls in fact would consider him a violation in their company and they would certainly not want to fraternize in the company of a Troll. They are the very worst kind – smelly, abusive and certainly not acceptable to entertain my girls, I can tell you that.'

'That doesn't exactly answer my question Drasilla – do you, or, do you not, harbor him in your establishment?'

'Oh alright, if you must be tiresome darling, but I can only say that I can answer any questions that you put to me when you physically attend here at my premises. I would like to see you for old time's sake anyway, so why don't we say around 8:00 pm tomorrow evening. We can have a cozy little chat together – how about that darling?'

'That sounds good to me although I would have preferred an earlier time within my regular official working hours,' he replied with trepidation.

'Oh come on now darling, I'm not going to bite you,' she said laughing.

'Now that's exactly what I am afraid of,' Errol replied smiling to himself.

'What exactly are you so afraid of, yourself or me?'

'I'm certainly not worried what I might do or not do; rather what you will do Drasilla – I know you so well and you have always got some sort of trick up your sleeve.'

'All righty then my darling, let's just make it a nice respectable evening. I would ideally like to invite you over for a dinner and if you bring your good wife with you, it would be all the more interesting.'

'Now look Drasilla, this is no time for a little social gathering; I will be attending at your premises purely on official business, as I have told you and I want to make that very clear to you – no funny business.'

'Oh shame, but I would like to invite you over for a bite to eat; that's the least I can do for you my darling. I never have people over without offering them my hospitality – but, if you are going to be such a bore about it, I would rather you didn't bother coming over at all.'

'Drasilla, I am not in the mood for your games but fine... I will come over for my official business and if you have dinner waiting for me, I will not be a bore, as you put it.'

'Good, then that's settled my darling,' she purred down the phone. 'I am so sorry I will not be able to meet your dear little wife. But, please do tell her that I just adore all her designs and if she would be so kind as to send me over one of her new catalogues I would be so grateful.'

'Fine, I'll bring one over – see you tomorrow at 8:00,' he answered gruffly before slamming the receiver down a little too sharply which he had not intended to do but one of his deputies was hovering around with a sneer on his face.

'Don't say a word,' he warned pointing his finger menacingly at the deputy now smiling a little too smugly for Errol's liking.

Drasilla placed the receiver down gently grinning like a Cheshire cat. She then reached over and picked up the receiver again. 'Cora, put me through to the kitchen please – I want to speak to Alice.'

She lightly tapped on the mouthpiece with her long talon nails painted a vivid bright red while waiting for Alice to come on the line.

'Hello Madam – what can I do for you?' Alice asked breathlessly having rushed from the kitchen to a phone on the wall in the adjoining lobby.

'Yes hello Alice, I would like you to arrange a sumptuous dinner for two tomorrow at 8:00. I would like to have the best steak served – rare of course and dripping with blood, succulent and juicy, and a bottle or two of our best full bodied red wine.

'I want it to be a very relaxing evening meant to soothe jangled nerves – some soothing music wouldn't go amiss either. I am expecting the Sheriff and we have to treat him extra special,' she continued.

'I will have everything under control Madam – you will not be disappointed. I know what the Sheriff likes to eat; he was a very popular guest here at one time and always enjoyed my cooking and I must say we have all missed him. I will be sure to have his favorite food to serve including corn on the cob, creamy potato salad with medium rare steak; he does like simple food.'

'Very good Alice – thank you. Please be sure to have plenty of Champagne on ice.'

'And how is Mr. Errol these days? We haven't seen him around here for an age now,' Alice added.

'Well, let's just say that he is a pillar of the community now and certainly not able to continue his life of vice.'

Chapter Eight

Drasilla made her way down to the lower level of the cave waving her silk diamond encrusted fan in front of her face; she was ready this time for any unpleasant smells likely to be swirling around the quarters occupied by Gilroy and Bogey. Her nose twitched in anticipation of foul smells that would assault the delicate membrane tissue of her nostrils.

Much to her surprise, the air was clear and still sweet smelling and she was amazed when Bogey opened the main door and bade her welcome into their lobby.

'Welcome Madam,' Gilroy gushed as he strode through from their lounge wearing an elegant smoking jacket made from the finest quality velvet in a rich burgundy colour, finished with traditional twisted cord.

'To what do we owe to this immense pleasure of your company in our humble abode,' Gilroy gushed as he bowed flamboyantly, a grin of pure delight spreading over his face.

'My, my, my, you do look elegant in your smoking jacket,' she said, as she stopped fanning herself. 'Can I detect an improvement in your hygiene – why you're almost like a new man.'

'Aye and it's all thanks to you Madam. I do feel like a new man,' he said extending his arms out wide towards her and breaking out into song laughing and singing somewhat out of tune as he spun pirouetting around the room powerless to prevent the occasional unintended outbreak of wind from his great behind, wafting out poisonous odours.

'♪♪♪ I feel gorgeous and oh so damn good-looking – I feel charming and witty and bright and I pity any Troll who isn't me tonight.

See that drop dead gorgeous Troll in that mirror there – who can that attractive Troll beeee – such a handsome face, such a charming smile, such a handsome meeee ♪♩♪.'

Bogey looked on in utter astonishment and now hastily turned his back on them both trying to suppress his laughter and pressing his hands over his ears to shut out the not so dulcet tones assaulting his sensitive ears – his body rocking; he tried desperately to hold his breath but the explosion of giggles burst out uncontrollably.

'I'm errr – so sorry,' he said snorting, bending over trying to hide his amusement at the farcical behaviour of his boss.

'Well, that is most entertaining Gilroy, I am lost for words,' Drasilla said quickly fanning herself again, also trying very hard not to laugh. It took a lot to amuse Drasilla but she had to admit to herself that this little show had far surpassed her expectations of being entertained.

'This is jusss foor you my most eloquent and d-delectable Madam hic hic hic – scuze me; I just adore you and I want to give you everything that you soo desire, my queen, my goddess, my darling Silla... I give you my all, my precious queen. I will rock you, I will rock you.' With that said he fell flat on his face, completely inebriated.

'Oh dear, what an earth has come over him – has he completely lost his mind?' Drasilla asked turning to Bogey.

'He's been under a lot of stress Madam and has just drunk six glasses of champagne straight down on an empty stomach.'

'Well, I had no idea that he was such a sensitive creature Bogey. But just throw a glass of cold water over him because I have some important information to share with him.'

'OK, Madam, I'll do just that,' Bogey said as he ambled into the kitchen for a jug of cold water. He quickly came back and threw the cold water directly onto Gilroy's face.

'Whaaat, I'll kill you... get away with you. I'll fight you to the very end for her hand; you'll not win my old friend for I am the stud that she craves for.' Gilroy mumbled as he sprang up from the floor with fists waving out in front of him and again slumping flat on his face still mumbling his adoration for his goddess.

'Look, I'll just come back Bogey; please tell Gilroy that I have some important news to discuss with him. But I must ask you to inform him that he must make himself scarce tomorrow evening as I have to entertain Errol, who is under the impression that I am harbouring a wanted criminal. I understand that he is referring to Gilroy and I must ask you Bogey to keep to this lower level as he may come with a warrant to search my premises.'

'I understand Madam; I will keep him quiet and I promise you that we will keep a low profile at all times tomorrow evening.'

'Very good Bogey – I know I can trust you to make him understand the importance of staying away from my level tomorrow evening at 8:00. If Errol suspects anything, he will be waiting for Gilroy to make a mistake. I need to talk to Gilroy anyway about the business and as I said I have some good news. But, in the meantime, I need him to behave himself and not make more of a fool of himself than he already is – sometimes I think that you are his boss and not the other way round Bogey.'

'I'll be sure to tell him that Madam... I mean, not about him being a fool but...'

'OK Bogey, no need to get yourself in a tangle – let's just leave it for now. Oh and by the way I need to go over some new designs of security uniforms with him; I have a catalogue to go through with him. He will need to be re-measured again as I fear he may well have put on a little extra weight around his middle. And, I insist that the Pug brothers are measured up for new uniforms also, I am tired of seeing them outside in their colourful hideous clothes. I need to see them looking more smart and professional befitting to their important function here in my empire.'

Drasilla smiled at Bogey as he opened the door for her and quietly closed it behind her. She had to admit to herself that she had grown very fond of both of them; they were both farcical creatures; Gilroy more so than Bogey but she had become accustomed to their antics.

Although it was the general opinion that Drasilla was a wicked vampire queen running a place of ill-repute, she was in fact a kind and generous person with a heart of gold. Her huge conglomerate, though mainly burlesque entertainment was fast becoming a popular health spa spot. Her whole reputation as a vampire queen was after all her own brilliant idea of an exciting theme for her burlesque shows and deep dark dungeon pleasure shows. To her absolute astonishment and delight she also discovered in and around the caves that there were hot springs and she had had the areas made into luxurious bathing areas. She was fast becoming the richest fairy in all the area.

Her entertaining part of the business was still thriving; her burlesque dancers were the most glamorous females gyrating in fishnet stockings and she took great pride in selecting the most beautiful of the girls brought to her; they were specially trained in the art of the magic of provocative burlesque dance.

She had employed Gerard, a well known experienced choreographer and director of erotic shows; he had trained as a ballet dancer at an early age but later had decided to become a choreographer of exotic dancing which he had become interested in during his travels throughout Europe. He was also a very strong and skilful gymnast and his dance routines and performances included exercises requiring physical strength, flexibility, power, agility, coordination and grace. When on stage Gerard always performed in high heels and his performances were sassy and mesmerising.

Gerard loved to practice his dance routines in the fresh air away from the darkness of the caves at times and often attracted a large audience of stragglers around the outside of the underground caves including the huge menacing Gluts and the tiny ridiculous looking Hobgoblin Pug brothers, who were always very curious at such displays of frivolous gyratory movements.

The Pugs were ugly little hobgoblin creatures who Drasilla had recruited to keep watch on the outside of her dwelling caves. They were in payment fed on scraps of food discarded from the kitchen. These small creatures were not particularly threatening as opposed to the Gluts, who were more of a danger. The Pugs could be tossed outside with one sweep of a hand when they became a nuisance. They were also very cowardly when not in huge groups. The Gluts were much more aggressive and treacherous; they were tall goon like creatures with long noses and were covered in a slimy substance, which if transferred to another being would weaken their ability to move and they would slowly shrivel up and cease to exist.

Gerard had many a time himself been circled by the Gluts and when they had advanced too close to him, he had no choice but to soar into the air practising one of his ballet routines to escape their venomous touch or suffocation by their sudden burst of green putrid glob.

Gerard often felt completely irritated when his rehearsals where disrupted by such unwholesome creatures. On this particular day when he noticed the ugly Pug brothers loitering around, he suddenly lashed out at them viciously with his high heeled dancing shoes, giving vent to his rage.

They quickly scuttled away terrified, their eyes nearly popping out of their heads. He had to laugh to himself at this as they all looked so comical in their puzzled state trying to clamber over each other in their haste to escape from his angry outburst, their small bloated bodies making it hard for them to move swiftly.

Chapter Nine

Clancy, a teenage Hobgoblin, the oldest of the Pug brothers was a particularly ugly little form with a tall sprout of green fuzz on the top of his head which he kept hidden under a large pointed cap; his bloated tummy protruded out making it difficult for him to walk straight and he constantly toppled over his own feet. He was an absurdly merry gay Hobgoblin and spent all his time prancing and mincing around the woodlands in his little pink flip flops with his younger brothers Cedric and Cecil, who were both equally ugly, although Cecil had a glass eye which often popped out without warning. All the Pugs had huge bulging eyes giving them a goggled-eyed appearance.

They scrambled off panting loudly towards a large tree to hide out of sight from Gerard and his treacherously high spiky heels.

'Darlings, that great sulking magnificent creature is having one of his tantrums and as much as I absolutely adore watching him, I'm off if you two little popsicles want to come with me – I am tired of getting my delicate arse kicked by his great sequined high heels,' Clancy told his brothers huffing and puffing dramatically as he held one hand against his brow. 'He makes me feel positively unwanted. Ooh, I tell you darlings, he is so aloof; he's got a face like a smacked arse – if he wasn't so stand offish, he would be my kind of man,' he continued flicking his head causing his little pointed hat to topple off.

'If Drasilla catches sight of us slinking off like this, you will be feeling her boot up yer backside instead and the force of that will send us straight back to the wasteland area where all the vultures live and where will that leave us. I'll tell you, once we get outside on our own, Gilroy will be onto us as quick as lightning – and, you know what that means; we will be smoked crackle,' Cedric replied.

'I'll tell you what we will do darlings,' Clancy said, again huffing and puffing dramatically while pointing his bent misshapen knobbly finger at Cedric, 'We will wait behind that tree over there while all the others scramble all over around , making complete idiots of themselves. It's a complete waste of time and energy even trying to get near him – he just whacks us over the head and sends us flying from one end of the garden to another – positively gives me a headache every time.'

'Quick come on you two – get a move on,' Clancy said impatiently, suddenly whacking Cecil on the back of his head, causing his glass eye to pop out, flying off into the dried out grey moss all around on the ground.

'You idiot,' Cecil cried out, 'Look what you've done now,' he said throwing himself onto the ground frantically groping around trying to find his glass eye.

'Leave it now, you boggled-eyed dozy looking mutt; I've had enough of you both – you slow me down; I simply can't think straight with two idiot brothers like you. Oooh, you make me that nervous, I can promise you that. We'll come back and look for your eye when he has gone. I've still got the bruises on my delicate behind from that last kicking I had. I'm not going to be hanging around for more insults and Pug bashing – it's positively Pug abuse darlings,' he said as he jerked his head back again dramatically.

'But I'm going to give it my all,' said Cedric panting as he danced around boxing into the air. 'I'll not be ordered around by a dancing poof – I'll not let a sequined pansy get the better of me. COME ON YOU BAG OF SEQUINS – I'LL SHOW YOU WHAT WE ARE MADE OF – MAKE MY DAY. SHAKE MY BOOTY,' he yelled into the air.

Clancy looked at him in astonishment, quickly losing his patience as he whacked him around the back of his head. 'What on earth has gotten into you? For goodness sake stop acting like a complete moron –

you're making me that nervous, I am sweating like a pig.'

'Why don't you just move on and get lost you bunch of cream puffs; you useless slobbering cowards – or else you will be feeling my great boot more likely,' said Glob, the most feared of the Gluts. He was considered to be the most pleasing to look at of the whole tribe although, like the other Gluts, he was hideous beyond belief. His nose was especially longer than the others which gave him a superior sense of smell and he actually had some hair on the top of his head, unlike all the others who were completely bald.

The Pug brothers all spun around in horror as he stood behind them.

'Who, who, who are you calling a bbbunch of cccream pppuffs? You, you great goon-faced bag of mucous and tttalk about the kettle calling the pot bbblack,' Cedric stuttered visibly trembling, trying to stand as tall as his little fat body would allow him and then suddenly losing his bravado and ducking behind Clancy.

'Don't you mean the pot calling the kettle black,' Cecil said out of the corner of his mouth.

'That's what I just said,' Cedric muttered still hiding behind Clancy.

'Shush you two – are you asking for trouble; are you trying to get us spit slaughtered,' Clancy hissed at him, elbowing Cedric sharply in his ribs.

'Oooh, now ducks, don't get your knickers in a twist,' Clancy said nervously, smiling coyly at Glob. 'Yes, we do agree with you, sweetie pie – no doubt about it, we are useless cowards and are certainly a waste of space – so if you don't mind we'll be off,' Clancy continued, also visibly shaking in his boots.

With that, Glob let out a vicious snarl that rendered the brothers quivering with fear, his onslaught of mucous missing them by inches.

'Quick, come on, let's get out of here before he spits at us again – he's another one with a face like a smacked arse,' Clancy whispered to Cedric and Cecil, slowly backing away.

Without so much as a farewell and attempting to appear as nonchalant as they possibly could, they slowly backed away in the opposite direction towards another larger tree trying to create as much space between themselves and Glob as they could. They did not want to be this day's light snack to Glob and his pack of flesh eating demons.

'Didn't I tell you sweetie pies that we were better off hiding behind a tree with all that arse kicking going on,' Clancy told his brothers as he now resumed his attention on Gerard.

'Why he is positively so mean and strong – oooh, I tell you,' he continued pouting, his eyes twinkling with delight at the sight of Gerard.

'Oh stop yer jabbering and drawling, will ya,' Cecil whispered. 'And, don't you be forgetting about my glass eye.'

'Yes, yes, sweetie pie, we can have a good look later – just let me watch this magnificent creature a little bit longer,' Clancy said, visibly dribbling at the sight of Gerard pirouetting around.

Clancy had a secret desire to dance like Gerard and he stood there with stars in his eyes picturing himself and his brothers in a small dance troupe wearing sequinned high heels, just like Gerard.

'I just want to be sick,' Cedric said as he pulled Cecil up by his ear from the side of Clancy. 'Let's get out of here – just leave that simpering fool on his own to drawl over whatsisname over there prancing around like a big girl.'

'What about that other great skulking muscle bound freak Dargo; only last week you were besotted by him and drawling at the mouth,' Cecil said as Cedric was dragging him along by his ear.

'Oh but that was last week darlings – out of sight, out of mind but I just adore them both, such magnicent creatures. I tell you I just adore them, don't you know', Clancy said visibly swooning at the sight of Gerard.

'Yes, you have made your feelings perfectly clear. What I know brother of mine, is that you are delusional, you need to look into a mirror every day to check your true identity; you will see that like us, you are just a weird looking inconspicuous creature,' Cedric said rolling his eyes.

'And I love you too little brother of mine,' Clancy answered laughing.

Chapter Ten

It was a glorious bright summer morning with flowers abloom and birds singing joyously outside. Shimmers of sunshine streamed in through her bedroom window as Claudette awoke feeling all the joys of spring.

Claudette was a pretty young peasant girl with long flaming red hair cascading down her slender back and big green eyes. She lived in the thick of the woodlands in a nearby village called Hemlock, in a small cottage with her godfather, Gruntle, an old grisly absentminded leprechaun Wizard.

Gruntle was extremely kind and gentle and was respected by all who dwelled in the woodlands and nearby villages. It was understood that he had stumbled upon Claudette when she was a tiny baby, left by a miniscule silver fairy angel in the thick of the woodlands enshrouded in stardust to protect her. It was said that he had gathered the tiny bundle in his arms, wrapped her in a blanket of autumn leaves and had carried her back to his small cottage bound to nurture the small abandoned child.

It was believed that Gruntle was very rich and had many treasure crocks hidden away, but he preferred to spend his time working as the herbalist for the areas and could cure minor ailments although he liked folk to think that he possessed great magical powers.

The old man's beard and hair was a rusty red colour like autumn leaves – the former descending almost to his girdle. His thick over-grown brows jutted out above his still piercing blue eyes that crinkled when he smiled. His forehead was high and ploughed by innumerable wrinkles. His attire consisted of a long loose brown sack cloth with a thick leather girdle bound around his middle and his head was covered by a cap, from beneath which his grisly hair cascaded over his shoulders. Indeed his rusty coloured hair and long beard gave him a look of an old overgrown nutty professor.

Nobody knew exactly how old he was but they knew that Wizards lived for hundreds of years. He was neither bent over nor hobbled along but he always walked with an old rickety wooden walking stick which sometimes spoke to him as he marched along through the woods with great swiftness like a younger man.

Claudette would reach the age of 16 years this next day and she knew that Gruntle had planned a forest celebration for her with all the magical fairies and small animals to join in with her – she was looking forward to it.

She was feeling particularly good these days and had noticed a sparkle in her eyes and, well, maybe it was just her imagination, but she could swear that tiny sparks of silver stardust sometimes ignited from her fingers when she touched flowers and such foliage and it was as if the plants stood to attention and seemed to bloom radiantly before her very eyes.

She sprung out of her small wooden bed and hurriedly pulled the flowery bedspread neatly back into place. She loved her room; the windows were adorned with floral patterned curtains and the walls were full of pictures of all her small fairy friends. She had the most charming small dresser next to her bed upon which sat a wooden mirror especially carved for her by Gruntle.

She peered into her small mirror while she was dressing feeling pleased with the image she reflected. Although she thought herself somewhat plain with her pale freckled complexion, she loved her long flaming red hair which she considered her crowning glory. She proudly tossed her head back and then patiently wove her hair into two neat plaits at each side; her hair was so abundant that it was almost like two pieces of rope hanging down each side of her face.

'I'm not too bad at all; just a little bit scrawny,' she told her reflection as she swung her two ropey plaits from side to side. 'At least that's what Gruntle is always telling me; but I think that on the whole, I am very nice-looking. Yes, I really do think that I am pretty and charming,' she continued as she begun to twirl around her room humming to herself.

'What's going on in there,' she heard Gruntle yell through her closed door. 'Is it a baby elephant living in there that I know nothing about,' he said as he knocked on her door to enter.

'Ooooh you, you know fine well that it is not a baby elephant and if it was it would be a scrawny one,' she replied giggling.

Gruntle then blundered through the door and scooped her up twirling her around the room until she begged him to stop and they both slumped to the floor laughing.

Claudette lived a somewhat carefree life and spent her days picking herbs and spices for Gruntle to make the various medicines he kept in his small workshop next to his cottage. He catered for the old goblins who came to him with their aches and pains, the many elfins, pixies and fairies when they had a sickness and of course the small injured animals.

On this particular day after Claudette had left wearing her very best bonnet, Gruntle had decided to go out into the woods himself as he planned to collect flowers to make an arrangement of dried flowers carefully placed in a small basket as a gift for Claudette's birthday. He strode through the woods hoping that he would not run into Claudette which of course would spoil his surprise.

'You silly old codger,' said the old rickety walking stick that he always carried with him. He was an extremely grumpy walking stick and Gruntle mostly just deliberately ignored him as much as he could. They had been together for so long and he was after all, in his own way, very fond of the walking stick.

'I don't know why you drag me out every day like this in wind and rain; I get so muddy and cold sometimes; it's just not fair seeing as you can get along perfectly well without me,' he continued sighing loudly.

'Be quiet and stop your moaning, you are like an old record playing the same tune over and over again,' Gruntle replied, chuckling in his beard.

'I can't be bothered with you but out of the kindness of my heart, I like to take you along with me so that you will not become a stagnant and bent up old stick; well, much more of a bent up old stick than you already are. And besides I just like to aggravate you.'

'Yes, well, unlike you, I need my comforts in my decrepit old age and would prefer to loll up against a big warm fireside with my slippers. At my age I should be allowed to lounge around and relax – not to be dragged out into the wintery cold mornings according to your quirky mood.'

'Is this all the thanks I get; I try to give you a bit of exercise to shake the cobwebs out of your old rickety addled worm-ridden wooden brain – you cantankerous old fool,' Gruntle retorted. 'Next time, I won't bother. I'll leave you lolling around the fireplace until you become a dried up old charred twig.'

'How dare you speak to me like that; I who have been your rock of support – a loyal and thoughtful friend; that's me and you have never appreciated my support.'

'Huh, rock of support, is that how you see yourself – more like a rickety old prop that I don't really need,' replied Gruntle in mock indignation.

The walking stick suddenly spun around in his hand so that his face could not be seen by Gruntle.

'Huh, don't even bother to talk to me now,' he told Gruntle.

'Oh we are quite contrary aren't we? Well, fine, that suits me you obstinate old fool,' Gruntle replied.

Gruntle ambled around in complete silence as he collected as many wild flowers as he could. He knew that Claudette loved the heavy scented foliage and he was sure to pick as many plants and flowers as he could find. He decided he would also make her a flowery tiara adornment.

When he had finished his collection, he propped the walking stick up against a tree. He had also collected some apples and lounged languorously by the side of the tree in the sun, chewing on one while he passed away time idly in the glorious sunshine.

When he had rested his old body sufficiently he eased himself up by the side of the tree where he had reclined in a most enjoyable recumbent position, picked up his basket ready to amble off back to his cottage.

'Oih, yer silliness, aren't you forgetting something,' a voice rang out from behind him.

'Oh I thought you were not speaking to me,' Gruntle replied turning around to the walking stick still propped up against the tree.

'Listen you absurd old Wizard, I'm not going to hang around here playing little games with you – just get me back to the cottage and then you can do what you like, as long as you leave me alone in peace,' the stick answered angrily.

Gruntle knew when he had taken a joke too far with the walking stick. He was after all a very old stick becoming crankier as time went on.

Gruntle toiled long and hard during the day but his work was very satisfying to him and when he rested in the evenings, the hard lines around his eyes softened in the candle light when relaxing with his beloved Claudette.

As always they sat together by the fire in the evenings, content with each other's company, Gruntle smoking his pipe and Claudette cross stitching, completely unaware that their contentment was about to be threatened and compromised by a deadly foe.

Chapter Eleven

Dargo, a great magnificent god of the sky, half eagle, half man, lay there for a while in a state of half sleep, his mighty body stretched out on the withered cracked and dried out ground beneath and around him.

Dargo possessed the mighty strength of twenty men all in one and had special powers including changing himself into different images or rendering himself completely invisible to his foe, he was considered to be a great hero in the arca. He was a strikingly handsome man with white blond hair, piercing blue eyes and great silver white powerful wings.

He had suffered a terrible tragedy when his beautiful bride Petra and his tiny daughter Gilda had been cruelly abducted by the wicked Troll Warrior.

Petra had been the sunshine of Dargo's world; she had danced her way into his heart with her tumble of golden hair and huge brown eyes; she had been a vision of loveliness in his life. After her disappearance, Dargo had been like a wild beast relentlessly roaming around searching for his lost family. He was consumed with a ferocious rage and vowed to avenge the evil Troll Warrior.

He stirred and sat up flexing the muscles in his great silver white wings and began to stretch his arms out, yawning loudly. The air was cool and there was a soft breeze which instantly refreshed him. He squinted up at the blue sky shielding his eyes against the sun, his mouth was bone dry.

He shook himself and suddenly leapt to his feet, walked over to the stream and knelt down to drink the cool water and to bathe his face. He raised his sodden face from the stream and stared at his image reflected in the water.

'I am like a great ragged silver phantom of the skies now – I have to pull myself together,' he growled to himself as he ran one hand over the overgrown stubble on his chin.

He suddenly stood up from the edge of the stream, spread his great wings and swooped into the air, his magnificent body glistening as he soared through the sky. He felt an uncontrollable spurt of energy and a passionate urge to fly away as far as he could and never return. His powerful great wings flapped loudly as he glided through the clouds climbing swiftly higher and higher.

'You can't leave us,' he clearly heard a small voice imploring him, echoing in the wind. He halted in his flight and began to descend back down towards the stream. He looked around puzzled but there was nobody around. *Perhaps he had imagined the cry of anguish – it was a voice full of torment and suffering.*

How could he just leave and give up hope – he could never give up and stop searching for them although he could not rid himself of the dread that they were long lost to him now. He felt utter despair as he ran his fingers through his thick tousled hair.

He hunched over the stream again, gazing into the water with sadness. Where the sun used to glisten on the water, creating sparkling ripples of small dazzling rainbows, it now lay silent and still. As he raised his sopping wet face from the stream he saw a reflection of Petra his wife holding tightly onto their daughter in the stillness of the water – they both looked so frail and pitiful. The image disappeared as quickly as it had appeared and all he could see was his own ragged image once again staring back at him.

He flinched then as the water began to swirl rapidly and his image seemed to change before his very eyes and he felt his body shudder as if an unknown force had entered into his veins.

A change of persona seemed to wash over him and overcome him; he stood up struggling to fend it off but the dark force had penetrated right through to his very soul and he was powerless to halt it.

He suddenly threw back his head laughing out loudly as he now lowered himself down by the edge of the stream again – this time the reflection revealed a cruel twisted perverted smile on his face.

'You handsome devil you,' he told himself as he winked at his reflection, blowing a kiss and laughing out loudly again as he stood up.

'My God, whatever has come over him – I've never seen him quite like that,' said Vanessa, a female vulture sitting on the branch of a tree nearby.

'Away with you – you flying rats, yer bunch of mangy scavengers – clear off out of it before I flatten yer all. I've got an important task to carry out this morning and I thank you all not to interfere,' he yelled at them.

'Well, I must say he has never acted so mean in all the time I've known him; he is like a different being – if I didn't know better, I would say that he has finally lost his mind. I don't know what his problem is,' squawked Vincent, the leader of the pack of vultures. 'After all, we are only trying to make a living like everybody else,' he added.

'Yea, anybody would think we enjoy doing what we do,' said Vanessa, his mate. 'God forbid, after all, we have to eat stinking rotten flesh to survive and who else would want to do that.

'Ooh, you really turn me on when you talk dirty,' Vincent replied. 'Let's turn off here and find a nice warm spot to get physical.'

'Hey, you two, less of the smutty talk,' said Vladimir, Vanessa's brother.

They hastily flew off reluctantly but not before Vanessa could see from a distance a small form wandering along towards the stream advancing towards the now menacing figure of Dargo.

As Claudette strolled along in the warmth of the sunshine upon her cheeks, completely engrossed in the beauty of the morning, she failed to see Dargo at first until she heard a loud groaning sound. She stopped in her tracks and then she saw him laid out prostrate on the ground in a seemingly intoxicated state with his great white wings spread out, his mighty body glistening with sweat.

'Are you OK,' Claudette called out.

At the sound of her voice Dargo attempted to rise up unsteadily before falling flat on his face again.

He appeared to be sleeping quite peacefully now with a smile on his face. As she knelt down next to him peering intently into his face, Dargo opened one eye slyly and chuckled under his breath – she immediately drew away startled.

A lovelier creature than he could ever imagine. Her figure was slight but tall and ravishingly perfectly proportioned, with a slender waist and long graceful limbs. Her features were almost angelic with a complexion smooth and glossy like satin tinged with a slight bloom. Her eyes were the colour of radiant summer lavenders and abundant bright ginger tresses fell on her dainty sleek shoulders. 'Yes, she'll do nicely as a little side dish with her special stardust magical power,' he whispered under his breath still chuckling.

'Can I help you?' she now asked.

'Well if you insist kind maiden. Could you help me to my feet – I fear I've had too much sun this day and feel quite unsteady on my feet,' he replied sitting up and taking hold of her small hand in his.

'Yes, of course,' she told him as he staggered up holding onto her small hand tightly.

'It's so kind of you my dear,' he said as they began walking together in the opposite direction of where she had been going, his hand still firmly holding onto hers.

Chapter Twelve

Drasilla stood in front of her mirror admiring the way the exquisite shimmering damask coloured gown, designed by Labelle, accentuated her slender shape. It clung to her body and she had carefully selected this particular gown to soften Errol; he would be sure to forget himself and the importance of his visit. She would indulge him with a bottle or two of the very finest champagne and they would laugh about old times.

Her blue black hair shimmered like silk and her violet eyes smouldered – her skin was like velvet, rich and smooth. She stood there admiring her perfectly proportioned regal statuesque posture; her classical beauty and elegance was the envy of all women who came into her view. She was a vision of loveliness – a walking dream.

She was not a modest person after all and never had been; she knew what she wanted and would go to any length to own anything and everything she wanted; it was her entitlement after all in her very own monarchy.

When she was completely satisfied with her appearance, she opened her large jewellery box encrusted with pearls and gems and selected a pair of emerald garish earrings and a matching emerald choker. She stood back and admired the beautiful jewellery; she had collected some stunning pieces of jewellery over the years – all had been gifts from her many suitors over time.

Her boudoir and adjoining sitting room were an opulent array of rich decoration and colours of purples and sensual pinks. She had had it especially designed and it reflected her femininity, luxury and flamboyance. Amongst all the purple and pink, a splash of gold colours, beads and glass all brought a touch of mystery and extravagance and was perfect for capturing that sensual, sumptuous look, conjuring up a bohemian, romantic style.

Drasilla loved the feeling of sensuality and the shimmering organza materials and silks also added an air of mystery and glamour to her quarters. Her rooms were full of photographs of all the many suitors throughout the years that she had romanced in these very rooms and they had all loved her.

She walked over to her dresser and selected one of her bottles of sensual perfumes; she decided that she would wear one of her musk perfumes which she now sprayed all over herself including her hair.

She wore her hair piled on the top of her head in a beehive style and her makeup consisted of long glittering false eyelashes, ruby red lipstick and just a touch of rouge to give her chilling white skin a little glow.

Errol arrived on time, exactly at 8:00 pm, dressed in his sheriff's outfit which he knew would annoy Drasilla. He was led into her luxurious sitting room next to her dining parlour room by Claude, her chief footman.

'Please take a seat by the fireside while I inform Madam of your arrival,' Claude said as he handed Errol a glass of Champagne.

Errol accepted the glass of Champagne and took a sip while he sat by the roaring fireside; it was a cold evening and it was a welcome sight for him. He took another sip of the Champagne – he was after all officially off duty although he had every intention of treating it as official business. He had to admit to himself that he was looking forward to a good meal; he loved a good steak, cooked rare and succulent. The Champagne tasted excellent and he took another sip and then another when Drasilla came into the room almost floating in her magnificent body hugging dress.

'Hello my darling Errol – it's so good to see you,' Drasilla said as she rang the cord bell for Claude.

'I see you are enjoying a glass of Champagne; Claude will refill it for you as I see you have nearly finished your first glass, or is it your second darling?'

'It's good to see you too – I must admit I feel so relaxed; I've been up to my eyes in my work. Apart from everything else, I've been refurbishing our small cottage and it is taking up all my spare time so I am so in need of some relaxation.'

'Oh, there you are Claude, please refill Errol's glass,' she said as she took a glass of Champagne for herself from the tray Claude was carrying.

'Yes, Madam and Mildred says that everything is laid out for you when you are both ready to eat.'

'We'll maybe just be around 20 minutes and then we will come through to eat – thank you Claude and please bring through another bottle of Champagne.'

Claude nodded as he bowed to her but before walking out of the room he hesitated for a moment and turned to look at Errol with a strange expression on his face.

Errol turned and caught Claude staring at him attentively; he frowned as if silently questioning him but Claude quickly turned and left the room.

'Is he OK?' he now asked Drasilla. 'He gives me the creeps and makes the hair on the back of my neck stand up.'

'Who, my darling?' answered Drasilla.

'Claude, he was staring at me as if I had two heads.'

'Now darling don't start that; I know you have episodes of paranoia but let's give that a miss this evening – it's far too exhausting for me to have to deal with you in that state,' Drasilla said turning to Errol with a glint of annoyance in her eyes. 'Never mind about Claude staring at you, I'm going to stare at you now and I want you to think very carefully about what I told you not to do.'

'I know – I know what you are going to say Drasilla and I'm sorry but I just didn't have the time to go home and change,' he replied apologetically, smiling but clicking his tongue as was his habit when he was slightly agitated.

'You know how I hate that uniform darling and I do know without a doubt that you deliberately wore it to annoy me – now didn't you darling; you know I absolutely detest that awful uniform. I hope you didn't forget to bring me a copy of your wife's latest catalogue.'

'You know me so well Drasilla – I wanted you to be sure that I am here on business but now that I am here I am determined to enjoy your company – I promise you, I will not be a bore and talk business the whole time. And, no I did not forget to bring you the catalogue,' he replied as he handed it to her.

'I should think so darling,' she said as she took the catalogue and sat down directly in front of him ready to flick through the pages.

'As you can see I've made a great effort to dress up for you and as you may have noticed, the dress is one of your wife's designs and I must say it is a beautiful design – one of her best.'

'I'm not sure whether you are trying to soften me up Drasilla – I know how cunning you are when you want your own way. I know you are up to something.'

'Why Errol, my darling man – how can you possibly think such a thing of me. That is so ungentle manly of you to call me cunning, as if I could or would behave in such a way. And, by the way, I suspect you didn't go home to change because you didn't want your wife to know that you were visiting me.'

They both laughed as Claude returned with another bottle of Champagne in an ice cooler bucket and placed it on the coffee table between them.

Errol immediately turned to look at him but Claude now kept his eyes downcast. Errol couldn't possibly swear to it, but he was almost sure that he detected a sinister and foreboding smirk on Claude's face and he was almost certain that Claude was chuckling ever so quietly to himself as he left the room.

'Now, what can I do for you my darling Errol; let's talk business now because I do not want to be spoiling our sumptuous meal with your work talk.'

'Well, as I've told you Drasilla, we have been conducting a thorough search for Gilroy, the notorious fairy collector or as some people call him, the Troll Warrior and have been receiving information that he has been hiding out in your expansion of caves. I have a search warrant which as you may or may not be aware is a court order issued by a magistrate, judge or Supreme Court official that authorizes law enforcement officers –

that's me, to conduct a search of a person, location, or vehicle for evidence of a crime and to confiscate evidence if it is found.'

'Huh, I can hardly believe that Gilroy could possibly be perceived as a Troll Warrior, why he is such a comic figure. I hardly think he could be considered as an evil menacing predator,' Drasilla said laughing.

'So, how do you know so much about Gilroy when you normally profess to not knowing anything about him?'

'My my, we are serious, aren't we my darling Sheriff and there's me thinking that you were intent on having a relaxing evening.'

'Well partly Drasilla, but as I was saying, we do have information that Gilroy has been seen in the vicinity of your dwellings. As an officer I do have the right to enter a property where a wanted person or persons has illegally sought shelter. '

'What I would like to know is, who is saying that Gilroy has been seen in my premises and what evidence does this person, or persons have,' Drasilla said as she stood up and refilled his Champagne glass.

Just then the most soothing music flooded the room and changed the whole mood for them both. Errol immediately became more relaxed and began drinking the Champagne again.

Drasilla winked at him as she stood. 'Shall we go through for dinner my darling – your favourite food is served up for you.'

Errol stood up and Drasilla linked her arm through his as they walked through to the dining area.

'Now isn't this so nice my darling – I do so enjoy your company and we have all missed you so much,' she purred as she laid her head on his shoulder as they walked towards the table.

'I must admit that I've missed your company too,' he said as he sat down at the table.

'Well, you are always welcome to dine here when you want my darling and it goes without saying that your wife is welcome to come with you,' she said laughing.

'I don't really think she would appreciate an invitation Drasilla – much as she would be so proud to see her designs worn so well by your many young models here, I think!'

'Tuck in my darling, there is plenty of everything,' she said as Claude served up the steak, potato salad and corn on the cob. 'It's very basic but I know that it's your favourite – none of that cordon bleu food for you.'

'Yes, well as long as it's not one of your Ox Tongue dishes braised in deep and full bodied red wine with mushrooms.'

'Oh darling, you are so squeamish – and you being a sheriff,' she said laughing.

'Talking about red wine, did you bring a couple of bottles of Cabernet Merlot red from our wine cellar Claude?'

'Yes Madam,' he answered as he poured the rich full bodied wine into their glasses.

'Not too much for me,' Errol said as he cupped his hand over the top of the glass. 'I think I've had quite enough to drink and if I am not careful I am going to go off into a deep sleep after this meal.'

'Oh come now darling, just enjoy – let's be merry,' Drasilla said laughing.

As he took his hand away from the glass Claude immediately filled it with the rich red wine, full to the brim. The last thing Errol remembered after eating his meal was that he felt very light headed and after watching one of Drasilla's burlesque shows, everything after that became a fuzzy blur and he felt all warm and at peace with the world.

Chapter Thirteen

Errol woke with a start unsure of where he was. He sighed with relief when he could see his wife Labelle standing over him gently shaking him as he laid slumped out on their sofa.

'Wake up lover boy – I hope you realize you are going to be late for work,' she said as he opened one bleary eye, trying desperately to focus on her.

'Ooooh my head, where am I,' he said moaning, his voice rasping, hardly audible.

'You are home with your wife – do you remember me?' she said laughing.

'Dargo dropped you off early this morning and left you on the couch where I decided to leave you to sleep it off. But anyway, I've called my office to say that I will be in a bit later. I'm going to prepare you a hearty breakfast but let me first give you something to take for that heavy head that you have and then I want you to go straight into the shower.'

Errol was a very attractive man; very tall and masculine – admirably proportioned. He had unruly dark brown wavy hair and smouldering black/brown eyes that seemed to twinkle when he smiled, which he often did. Life was very good for Errol; he seemed to lead a perfect and charmed existence, especially since he had become a married man.

Errol had on first sight been completely love struck by his new bride Labelle, the Queen of the Gothic fairies. Labelle had previously lived in parts of the woodland hexed and tainted by black magic. The other fairies teased her although only light heartedly, probably in fear and often called her Gothic Rose as she was always dressed in scantily clad tunics, her own designs, made of black feathers and blood red rose coloured taffeta. She had beautiful black lacy wings which she dusted with gold speckled powder.

When Errol and Labelle married, they had a sumptuous feast outside in the woodlands and all who lived in the woodlands and nearby villages had celebrated their joining of hearts – It had been a joyous occasion. It had been a wedding with a difference as all the guests came in fancy dress and all garments had been especially designed and made by the bride.

Labelle had been a beautiful bride and had worn one of her own designs; she had worn a red wedding dress decorated with beads and crystals which had a sweetheart taffeta corset also detailed with crystals. Her bridal gown was completed with a dreamy and romantic elegant red gauze wedding veil attached to a red rose tiara. She had carried a bouquet of exquisite blood red roses for a true fairy princess bride; the stems of which had been wrapped in silk French ribbon tied with a small ornate woven ribbon and bejewelled vintage ruby brooch.

As he now lay squinting up at her moaning in mock agony after his long night, she gave him a glass of bubbling honey dew elixir which he gratefully drank straight down and then hauled himself out of the sofa towards the bathroom for a long hot shower.

When he came out of the shower completely refreshed, he quickly dressed into a clean uniform lovingly placed on the bed ready for him and on smelling eggs and bacon cooking, he ran down the stairs into the kitchen. He was famished now after his hot shower and felt as if he could eat a horse.

He sat down at the table while Labelle poured out a mug of steaming hot coffee which he drank immediately and then tucked into the hearty breakfast of eggs, bacon, mushrooms, tomatoes and toast.

'Oh this is wonderful – just what I need,' he said gulping down huge mouthfuls. 'And, your magical elixir worked wonders for me – my headache has completely gone and I feel like a new man.'

'Yes, well if you must go out drinking all hours of the night, what do you expect?' Labelle said with a little knowing smirk on her face.

'Yes, well, I don't know about drinking – I'm sure something was put into one of my drinks because I must have gone out like a light during my meeting. Normally, as you know, I wouldn't drink while on duty but it was outside my normal working hours and I just thought, what is the harm in one or two drinks? But, anyway, now I will have to return to carry out the questioning I meant to do in the first place, which I obviously did not get around to.'

'Well, look, I'll have to go now but let me know what you have planned this evening and if you are coming straight home, I'll cook something nice for dinner,' she said as she quickly kissed him ready to go out of the door.

'Oh, your lips taste like eggs and bacon,' she said laughing and then she was gone out of the door.

Errol was slowly feeling better as he resumed gulping down his breakfast. When he had practically polished his plate and sat back sipping his second cup of coffee, there was a loud knocking at his door. He stood up, marched out of the kitchen and opened the front door to a very frantic Gruntle standing there waving his arms about.

'You've got to help me, Claudette has gone missing and rumour is that she had been abducted by Gilroy, the fairy collector. I have been beside myself since yesterday afternoon – I've been searching for her everywhere. I've looked everywhere and I am out of my mind with worry,' he lamented as he sank to the ground holding his aching head.

Errol leaned over and helped him back on his feet and pulled him through the door.

'Come inside and sit down, you've obviously not had any sleep and just need to sit for a few minutes. Let me pour you a strong cup of coffee while you tell me everything.'

Gruntle allowed himself to be guided into the kitchen and he slumped into one of the chairs as Errol poured him a cup of coffee which he gulped straight down.

'Tell me what happened from the start. When did you last see Claudette and what time did she go missing approximately as far as you know?'

'As usual she went out picking herbs and flowers like she always does every day and when she didn't come back I was beside myself with worry and went out looking for her. I know sometimes she wanders too far and, as you know, talks to everybody she sees practically, but, but, but ...' he began stuttering in his frantic state of mind.

'Take it slowly, just breathe,' Errol told him.

'Yes, phew, I am that out of breathe, I can hardly think straight but anyway as I was saying when she did not come back by the evening, I was worried out of my mind and went looking for her. Some vultures that I ran into said that they had first seen her being led away by Dargo, who they said, appeared to be in a disorderly state and behaving very mean......' He suddenly broke down and his head dropped between his knees.

'I really don't know what to believe – I just know that Gilroy is behind this. If he harms her, I don't know what I will do; I will want to kill him of course – you've got to help me Errol,' he continued close to collapse.

'And, what happened after that?' Errol asked impatiently.

'That's what I want to know – I don't know what happened after that,' Gruntle barked back at him.

'What I am trying to say Gruntle is, WHAT exactly did they mean, when they said they FIRST saw Claudette with Dargo?'

'Oh yes, I see what you mean – well, one of the vultures swore that he then saw Gilroy leading her away quite soon after. But it was from a distance and he wasn't exactly sure that it was Gilroy,' Gruntle replied looking vague.

'I thought you said that he could have sworn that he saw Gilroy,' Errol said.

'Don't confuse me – I can't think straight,' Gruntle barked at him.

'Give me a minute or two – I just need to call the station and let them know that I am following up on this and we can be out of the door,' Errol said patting Gruntle on the shoulder. 'We'll get this sorted out Gruntle – just take it easy.'

After he had called his station, he seemed to have a determined expression on his face giving Gruntle every confidence that he knew exactly what to do.

'I know that Gilroy is somewhere in the caves and that's where I believe we will find Claudette. I will call Drasilla now but I doubt very much that she will give me any information at this stage, but let me give her a call now,' he said as he picked up his mobile again.

He heard a constant ringing tone but as there was no subsequent answer, he then tried calling the servant's quarter and was then informed that Madam was out and they didn't know when to expect her back.

Just as he was about to put the mobile back in his back pocket it rang and when he answered, it was Dargo telling him that he had been informed that he was supposedly seen in the woods in a disorderly state prior to the disappearance of Claudette.

'Well Errol, you know that I have the occasional drink of Elderberry wine but I never overdo it and I was certainly not drinking on that particular day. I'm telling you Errol that was not me... so, what is going on here? I didn't even see Claudette in the woods.

As Errol had the mobile on loud speaker, he turned to look at Gruntle who was looking bewildered and disorientated.

'Well – look Dargo, let's get this sorted out. Can we meet you within the next twenty minutes somewhere private so that we can try to come up with an explanation?'

'What do you make of that?' he asked turning around to Gruntle as he hung up. 'That is very strange but as you know, Dargo and myself go back a long way and I know he would not lie about such a thing. Dargo would never get into a drunken and disorderly state like that; in all the time I've known him he has always been a gentleman.'

'Well I did think at the time that it was out of character for him to behave like that, but I'm telling you there is no mistaking Dargo – I mean, those vultures were absolutely adamant that it was him with Claudette to begin with. Mind you, the state he was allegedly in – I'm not at all surprised that he doesn't remember anything. But the vultures were positive that it was Dargo for sure as strange as he was behaving.'

'Come on then, let's go meet Dargo now – I suggested that we meet at his cottage.'

As they went through the door Errol was frowning; his thoughts were on his own behaviour the evening before and he now felt a little ashamed and alarmed that he too had also been in a somewhat disorderly condition and had been literally carried home. It seemed very strange to him now, when he really thought about it, that his wife had mentioned that Dargo himself had brought him to their door this same morning.

Chapter Fourteen

When Errol and Gruntle arrived outside Dargo's front door, Gruntle was feeling somewhat dubious about the whole situation – nothing seemed to add up. Dargo had in general been acting very suspiciously of late and there had certainly been many contradictory stories about him since he had lost his whole family some time ago, but could he do such a thing. It was very clear though that he had practically become a recluse.

When Dargo heard Errol and Gruntle outside, he strode to the door and quickly opened it. He looked from Errol's face to Gruntle's and immediately felt that they were less than willing to trust him.

'How are you feeling today?' asked Gruntle. 'Considering that you could hardly stand up yesterday,' he added discourteously.

'Who told you that?' Dargo asked looking puzzled.

'Look Dargo, we are not here to accuse you of anything at this stage but we do need to know how you are coping these days; it seems that you have been acting very strange of late. We do realize that it has been a long time since the disappearance of your family but we have been hearing some worrying reports about your behavior at times.'

'Come in and let's sort this out,' Dargo said frowning as he stood aside to let them through.

Gruntle immediately recognized a small basket and a little pink bonnet in the corner of his sitting room although he did not instantly react. Claudette always took this small basket into the woodlands to collect flowers or herbs.

'I'm just having some coffee, would you both like to join me?' Dargo asked as they both sat down on his large comfortable sofa.

They both accepted and when he went out into his kitchen to pour the coffee Gruntle pointed to the basket.

'This isn't looking good Errol – that's Claudette's basket and I know she had it with her when I last saw her and that is the pink bonnet she was wearing, so what is it doing here. It all looks very clear to me.'

'Let's not jump to any conclusions – it would be just so simple to point the finger at him, but I'm willing to give him the benefit of the doubt and give him the chance to explain himself,' Errol replied.

'How much benefit of the doubt do you need to give him – the evidence is right there staring at us,' Gruntle said rocking back and forth on the sofa almost unable to contain himself from leaping up and attacking Dargo.

'Would you keep your voice down – as I said we have to give him the chance to explain himself,' Errol repeated.

'Yes, but how do you explain his behavior yesterday – according to those three vultures, he really was two sheets to the wind and behaving very badly,' Gruntle replied.

'Me behaving very badly!' Dargo exclaimed as he strode back through from the kitchen with three mugs of coffee on a tray. 'And pray do tell me how I was behaving badly, particularly since I did not see either of you yesterday!' he added laughing.

'Of course you don't remember... and this is certainly no laughing matter Dargo so do not try my patience. You were observed to be laid out in the forest, two sheets to the wind and you were seen to go off hand in hand with my Claudette yesterday afternoon,' yelled Gruntle at him, hardly able to contain his temper.

'I'm sure that I would have remembered something about that even if I was two sheets to the wind; I'm telling you I don't have any recollection of seeing Claudette yesterday – I'M TELLING YOU,' Dargo persisted looking from one to the other.

As Errol sat there listening to these two men going back and forth with accusations and denials, he suddenly realized something that his wife had said to him just before she left for work; she had said that Dargo had dropped him off in the early hours of the morning.

'Just a minute you two, something has just occurred to me; something my wife told me this morning. I had been out most of the night on a business engagement and she told me that I had been brought back home in a drunken disorderly state myself by you Dargo – I'm a little confused about all this and am wondering what's going on here?'

'Right you two; I've had enough of this. In the first place, as I have already told you, I did not see either one of you yesterday or this morning. I had dinner here in my home yesterday evening and I went to my bed fairly early,' Dargo said indignantly.

'Then how do you explain that basket and bonnet over there,' Gruntle suddenly stated not able to restrain himself any longer; his hands on his hips looking very grim, pointing to the basket in the corner of the room.'

'What basket and bonnet,' Dargo said looking baffled.

'That basket and bonnet over there – Claudette wears that bonnet and takes that basket out every day to collect her flowers,' Gruntle quickly replied.

'I've never seen that basket or bonnet before,' Dargo answered. 'They were certainly not here yesterday when I came back from the woods.'

'So you were in the woods yesterday afternoon,' Errol said.

'I didn't say that I wasn't in the woods yesterday afternoon,' Dargo replied indignantly.

'So now you are saying that I abducted Claudette?' he added looking perplexed.

'Well not exactly Dargo. I don't really understand any of it at the moment, but it does seem very suspicious. Either you can't remember one day to another or we have a case of misguided identity here,' Errol said, his expression of displeasure and concentration causing him to frown. 'Are you telling me that you did not take me home during the early hours of this morning?'

'Not unless I was sleepwalking,' Dargo answered. 'This is the Troll Warrior that we are dealing with here, I am sure of that – he has taken Claudette and we have to find out where he has taken her.'

'I think you just want us to think that you can't remember anything just to avert the suspicion of guilt from yourself,' Gruntle murmured through gritted teeth.

'Let me just check back with Drasilla first before we do anything,' Errol said frowning again. I am now also remembering how weird her butler was acting during my meeting with her yesterday evening.'

'What meeting was that Errol?' Dargo quickly asked suspiciously. 'And just what has her butler got to do with it?'

'Yes, what has the butler got to do with it?' Gruntle asked looking extremely agitated still glaring at Dargo with sheer rage in his eyes.

'Well firstly, I am going to track down Gilroy the fairy collector and I have reason to believe that he is hiding out in Drasilla caves, and, secondly, I have reason to believe that her butler is involved somehow.'

'Don't waste your time looking for that idiot Gilroy – it's the Troll Warrior you should be looking for,' Dargo answered.

'As far as I am concerned, they are one and the same,' Errol said stubbornly as he stood up ready to leave.

'Where are you going,' Gruntle said. 'What are we going to do about Dargo? I want Claudette found and I want her found now,' he yelled. 'I can't bear the thought of her being held against her will. God forbid... if she is harmed in any way I will kill whoever is responsible,' he continued grinding his teeth.

'Calm down Gruntle, I will go straight back to see Drasilla and insist that she divulge Gilroy's whereabouts; I just know that she is keeping him somewhere safe in her caves.'

'I have a better idea – we'll all go to see Drasilla. At least we will all know where we all are at the same time, if that makes sense,' Dargo said scratching his chin.

'That's an excellent idea Dargo, because I want to keep my eye on you,' Gruntle said still glaring at him.

'I would imagine that Drasilla would be aware of all Gilroy's movements and she would certainly not accept the abduction of young maidens and keeping them imprisoned in her caves,' Errol said ignoring Gruntle's antagonistic defiant stare.

'Just a minute,' Errol said before stepping out of the cottage. 'What is that scratching sound coming from your loft?'

'What scratching sound?' Dargo asked looking up.

'I thought I heard something but never mind I expect it's just rats,' Errol said as he strode off in front of them out of the door

Chapter Fifteen

Gilroy was laid out on his chaise lounge resting in front of the TV; he really enjoyed the early part of the morning when he could just relax in his silk dressing gown sipping his Espresso coffee – the stronger, the better he enjoyed the rich taste.

He looked round as he heard Bogey ambling in groaning loudly; he had noticed of late that Bogey was becoming a tad overweight.

'My boy, I think you are putting on a little bit of weight around your middle; what you need is some exercise and I am sitting here thinking that we need to start using the gym here.'

'What do you mean – we? You are not seriously thinking that you are going to be going to any gym in your condition,' Bogey replied sarcastically.

'What do you mean in my condition, I'm not pregnant you know,' Gilroy replied indignantly.

'Many people will think otherwise – your stomach looks like you have swallowed a baby elephant.'

'You cheeky thing, let's have less of the insults – we are talking about your weight gain, not mine and I will thank you not to be so insensible to my feelings. I am quite aware that I am not blessed with such good looks and a well built strapping fit frame that females swoon over.'

'Oh, have I hurt your feelings now my lord. Anyway, I know I have put on weight and it is making me feel very uncomfortable so I am planning to start jogging every day – but, not today. I will start a brand new program tomorrow and wake up at the crack of dawn and start jogging and then I will join one of Gerrard's dance classes and before I know it I will be back to my slim and graceful self.'

'Never mind about all that,' Gilroy said as he pulled himself up to sitting position on his chaise lounge, where is that darn Claude this morning with our breakfast, I'm that hungry I could eat a horse. Go ring the bell for him, will ya Bogey baby, me old mate.'

Just then Claude came in pushing a food tray loaded with dishes of devilled eggs, bacon, sausages, mushrooms, toast, fruit juice and fresh coffee. The tray rattled as he seemed to stagger towards their dining table. In general he had a peculiar way of walking, but today it was almost like watching a drunken duck waddling along.

'Oh my God Claude, you look awful today – are you feeling unwell me old flannel?' Gilroy asked him.

'No Sir, I am not feeling very good at all today; my head is splitting and I have a huge lump on the back of my head as if I have been hit by a sledge hammer. And, I would thank you Sir not to call me your old flannel,' he replied wincing.

'Well alright me old fruit let me take a look,' Bogey said as he stepped behind him, grimacing at the greasy head of hair slicked flat against Claude's scalp, but sure enough there was a huge angry red lump looming out at the back of his head which Bogey proceeded to poke at.

'Ooooh,' screamed Claude. 'Please do not touch me Sir – that feels so painful.'

'You do have an enormous lump on the back of your head, it almost looks like a mini Claude head at the back there winking at me, but the question is how did it happen upon you,' Bogey continued as he recoiled back in horror and disgust from the greasy head as the lump suddenly spurted out some yellowish looking secretion.

'The little bogger spat at me,' Bogey grimaced.

'I am not at all sure how it happened upon me, but I do know that I was preparing myself to serve Madam as usual in the evening and then the next thing I knew, it was early this morning and I woke up in my thermal long johns on the floor in my quarters.'

'That must be the most horrible sight; I hope one of those pretty maids didn't come upon you in that state – it would be enough to give her the fright of her life. Are you sure you didn't partake in a little too much of Madam's wine before serving it up to her,' Bogey said sniggering.

'Yes, and then had some jiggy jiggy with one of her delectable burlesque dancers my friend,' Gilroy added pointing his finger at Claude. 'You naughty, naughty man you,' he said rubbing his hands together gleefully, his toothless mouth puckering up giving him a look of a perverted imbecile.

'I hardly think that this is a joke gentlemen, and, if you don't mind, I will be serving up your breakfast and then I will be on my way; I don't have the time to dally around and join in little light tête-à-têtes with you both this morning.'

'Oooh eerrr flower, we are a little rumpled and delicate today, aren't we – excuse us for wanting to enquire about your health and overall wellbeing Claude,' replied Gilroy sarcastically.

'Please just serve up everything to me as usual and I'll have another mug of hot coffee while you are about it,' Gilroy added.

'And I'll have the same Claude – but make it an extra large portion today, if you don't mind,' Bogey said.

'Oh no you won't, you'll have half the portions that I am going to have. Don't forget you are going on a diet today – just serve him up smaller portions than normal Claude.'

'No, remember what I was just saying Gilroy; I'm going to start my diet tomorrow after I have returned from an early morning jog. I will then have a miniscule breakfast followed by attending one of Gerard's dancing classes.'

Claude in the meantime served up two steaming hot plates of food for them both which he laid out on the dining table ready for them to seat themselves. As usual they both flew to the table nearly knocking over their chairs in the process in their haste to get to the table first.

On this particular day Gilroy had elbowed Bogey who had then stumbled onto the floor but quickly sprang up, picked up his chair and seated himself.

'You thought you could beat me to the table as usual Bogey baby, but I'm quicker than you and don't you forget it – you little rascal you.'

'Yes, but that won't be the case after I have started my fitness routine and just you wait, I'll be so fit and slim-line that I will move like lightning and leave you behind panting,' Bogey replied before stuffing his mouth with food.

Claude then ambled towards the door and before quietly closing the door behind him, he turned around to look at them both and rolled his eyes as he watched them both literally attacking the food, shoving great huge amounts of food into their mouths.

He then closed the door and shuffled off back towards the kitchen for his own breakfast. Gilroy very often insisted that he join them for breakfast and as much as he was tempted to at times, he did not relish the thought of all the eruptions of breaking wind from Gilroy throughout the meal – his nostril flared up just thinking about it.

When he got to the kitchen he found a message from Madam that she wanted to see him as soon as possible. He frowned in displeasure as he read the small note and noted that she had insisted that he go immediately to her office and that the matter was extremely urgent.

He hurried over to Madam's office, his throat was dry and he ached all over. He paused outside just before knocking but then he heard her immediately call to him to enter. She seemed to always know who was outside her office even before a person had the chance to knock – he found it positively disturbing and nerve racking. He stepped inside and immediately cast his eyes down; he was feeling hot, sweaty and very nervous.

'Well Claude and what have you to say for yourself after your appalling behavior yesterday evening. I must say I would have expected much, much more from you; you have proven yourself in the past to be a valuable part of my staff and someone that I could rely on and trust. But, after seeing you behave in such a strange and odd way, totally different to how I know and trust you. And, I must say I would never, never have believed that you would actually have such an extremely different and bizarre side to your personality.'

Claude stood there twitching and fidgeting on the spot, his eyes still downcast; he seemed unable to look her in the eyes.

'WELL CLAUDE, have you lost your tongue,' Drasilla now yelled at him.

Claude visibly jumped on the spot and his whole body seemed to leap to attention.

'Madam, I can only say that I cannot actually explain what exactly happened to me yesterday evening – all I can honestly say is that I wasn't entirely myself.'

'You can say that again Claude,' Drasilla replied frowning at him.

'Madam, I can only say that I cannot actually ...' Claude began to repeat again.

'That's enough Claude,' Drasilla said holding up her hand to cut him short mid way in his sentence, sighing in her impatience at his more than usual display of a dopey manner. Of course she knew only too well that there was nothing dopey about Claude; he just felt comfortable and safe casting himself such a role in his daily mundane life – it suited him to keep a low profile and if it appeared that he was docile and dopey, he was more than content with that persona.

'Don't pretend that you are more stupid than you look; I think I am beginning to see the real you. I just can't understand why you would act so disrespectful in front of Errol like that.'

When Drasilla's phone rang at that moment, she immediately waved her hand at Claude gesturing him to leave her office.

'We'll talk later Claude,' she said before picking up the receiver.

He nodded as he turned and stepped out of her office, his shoulders bent over more than usual. He was desperately worried about the events of the past evening – he could not remember a thing. *What on earth could he have done that was so displeasing,* he thought as he slowly closed the door to Drasilla's office.

'Yes, hello – who is it Clara?' Drasilla asked while lighting up one of her menthol cigarettes as she watched Claude slink out of her office looking extremely guilty.

'It's the Sheriff,' Clara replied.

'OK, put him through. Well, hello darling and how are we feeling this morning after your appalling behavior yesterday evening – you who are a well respected member of the community now,' she said with a note of disapproval in her voice.

'I'm sorry if I said anything or did anything inappropriate Drasilla but the Champagne seemed to have a disastrous effect on me and I wasn't exactly behaving myself. And, by the way, thanks for providing transportation for me; I understand Dargo drove me back home.'

'Well, disastrous or not Darling, I do forgive you – don't worry yourself about it – but I must admit I felt extremely anxious, especially when, well let's just say when...,' she paused, 'when you began to man-handle me. And, I have to say it took all my strength to fight you off.'

'Oh come off it Drasilla – don't come the shrinking violet with me; it won't wash with me lady. But anyway, I'm calling on a more serious matter though Drasilla. Claudette has gone missing and was seen last in the company of Dargo, but aside from that I do believe she has been abducted by Gilroy, otherwise known as the Troll Warrior; he has been up to his old tricks again Drasilla and this has got to stop. You must divulge his whereabouts – I know he has been hiding out in your caves for some time now.'

'That is terrible news but I have to say that in the first place Errol, Dargo did not drive you home. I gave strict instructions to Claude to drop you off although I have a bone to pick with him; he was also acting very suspiciously and in fact you actually complained about his behavior while you were here. I just can't understand it, he has always been such a reliable and trustworthy character and I have always been able to count on him for his faultless decorum.'

'Huh, whatever you say Drasilla – your household staff are all misfits and in my considered opinion, I wouldn't trust any of them as far as I could throw them especially your manservant Claude – I need to talk to him also. As I told you I found his behavior yesterday extremely suspicious.'

'Just what do you mean by that – I carefully selected all my staff not by who they were, or who I thought they were, but on my feminine instinct of their character – I have to say that I can sense a good person just by looking them in the eye and if they can stand in front of me without flinching, I know that they are truthful and trustworthy. But all said and done, I'm not asking for your considered opinion my darling – you've always totally lacked a sense of compassion and can never see beyond your own high standards. Not everyone is perfect like you and in your line of duty you should especially show understanding and a sense of compassion to others who are less fortunate than yourself.'

'I've no time for this lesson on my sense of morals Drasilla – as I've told you this is a serious matter; didn't you hear what I told you – Claudette has gone missing and Gruntle is frantic and nearly out of his mind with worry. I need you to tell me where I can find Gilroy.'

'Let me tell you something before I divulge the whereabouts of Gilroy, Errol my darling. Gilroy adores this unhealthy ghastly reputation that he has been labeled with, but in reality he is a kind misguided Troll who has had a very sad and unfortunate life and existence. If he has abducted Claudette and brought her here, don't you think that I would know about that, and, what about all the other victims that he has supposedly dragged off to some God forsaken place and kept captive until he decides to baste and bake them for his next meal.'

'Such as that may be, but we need to apprehend him.'

'Fine – do what you need to do,' Drasilla said exasperated by the whole subject; the day so far was beginning to look like a fiasco and she had half a mind to board her private plane and jet off to a faraway place to sun herself on a beach drinking several cool alcoholic cocktails but she knew that the combination would have a disastrous effect on her five hundred year old complexion.

'Thank you Drasilla, we are on our way – please do not say anything to either Gilroy or Claude to alert them in any way. And, please do not go anywhere else yourself,' he added as if reading her mind.

'Oh, am I now a suspect as well,' she replied haughtily.

With that said, Errol immediately and abruptly hung up his receiver.

Drasilla quietly replaced her receiver but sat there deep in thought.

'This is just so strange,' she said aloud pondering to herself, 'It seems to me that the whole evening was quite suspicious and I need to find out exactly what was going on.'

Chapter Sixteen

Claudette awoke suddenly shivering in the huge four poster bed; she had absolutely no memory of how she had been brought to wherever she was. The interior of the room was dark with only a few lamps glowing softly but she could see that it was a large imposing and oppressive room.

She sat up and swung her long legs over the side of the bed and ran to the window, drawing back the heavy curtaining to peer out. The bright sunshine nearly blinded her; she bent over and tried to open the small side window but it was locked. She blinked back tears in her eyes; she seemed unaware of what had actually happened to her and wandered around the huge room in a state of complete bewilderment.

'Were am I,' she gasped as she began to open adjoining doors leading to many cupboards and closets containing rows and rows of garments and shoes.

She ran back to the window pounding on the glass panel until her small fists hurt. She then ran over to the door but it was also locked and no matter how much she hammered on the door, nobody seemed to hear her cries for help.

'I have to get out of here,' she cried. 'Help me, help me,' she called out, but there was no answer and no sign of anybody coming to her aid.

Completely exhausting herself, she sank to the floor in a state of half consciousness. She could see a swirling mist in front of her eyes as she felt strong arms lifting her onto the bed and gently placing her head on the soft pillow.

'Hush, little girl, don't cry,' a soft voice whispered in her ear. She was weeping silently, there was fear and confusion in her, and her head was aching. He clasped her in the strength of his arms surrounding her with warmth and comfort, brushing her tumbling hair away from her face.

'I'm sorry I frightened you, my own dear child; my beautiful daughter. Go to sleep now.' He murmured the words against her temple, his lips brushing her forehead and then drawing up the bedspread around her to keep her warm and then he was gone.

She was bewildered by his words and sank into a deep heavy sleep and dreamed that she was running through a dark garden full of great musty black furry spider webs where she became trapped and when a huge spider with a human face began to scuttle towards her – she screamed and screamed. First it was the face of Gilroy intent on gobbling her up and then the face slowly turned into the face of Dargo, but in her dream he was an evil predator.

She awoke then thrashing around with beads of sweat pouring down her face, frantically brushing away imaginary spider webs from her face. She sprang from the bed and ran to the wash stand to bathe her face.

The cold water seemed to shock her out of her bleary state of mind and she began to feel calmer. After she had bathed herself, she selected a long warm robe and matching slippers, there were so many dresses to choose from; she had never seen so many before. *Where had they all come from and who did they belong to,* she found herself wondering.

She stood in front of a mirror and began to brush her unruly long tumbling hair and gasped when she saw that her hair had gone completely white. She shook her head, rubbed her eyes and squinted at her reflection thinking that she had not seen herself clearly.

'My hair,' she said with a sharp intake of her breath, barely able to breathe as she moved nearer to the small mirror above the washstand. 'It must be some sort of trickery of the light in this dark room,' she told herself.

But no, as she peered even closer into the mirror; so close that her nose almost touched the glass, she could clearly see that without a doubt her hair had changed from a vibrant red to a silvery white. She stumbled backwards and slumped back down on the bed in complete shock.

She rolled over on the bed and buried her face in the pillow as if trying to blot everything out from her mind.

She shook herself again, she was feeling so bizarre; she hoped and prayed that all this was just a horrible dream and that she would wake up and find herself back in her lovely little bedroom knowing that Gruntle was in the next room.

She sprang up from the bed again and walked towards the door which she found unlocked now and quietly opened it fearing that such an old heavy door would creak loudly and alert her abductor. She crept out of the room and ran down a spiral wooden stairway.

She stepped straight into a small cool shaded room where she could see French-windows wide open at the other end and when she walked through them she found herself in the garden that she had seen from the bedroom window.

The beauty of the garden was breathtaking. Sunlight filled the garden and she wandered amongst the sweet-smelling rose bushes, apricot trees and colourful flowerbeds, shrubs and lush green grassland – the smell in the air was intoxicating.

She could hear the birds singing and suddenly she felt almost happy and threw herself down on the ground and buried her face in a huge carpet of bluebells spread around, the wonderful smell of the flowers made her feel so lightheaded and carefree.

'Well my dear, I see that you have decided to explore my humble abode and what do you think of it – do you not think it is a most wondrous place to behold.'

Claudette turned and gasped as she looked up at Dargo; he was for sure the most beguiling man she had ever seen but now there was a slight hint of a wicked glint in his eyes and as he stood over her looking down at her, flashing a twisted smile at her, she felt a shudder spread over her body.

He held out his hand to her and as she clasped his strong hand, he drew her up from the bed of flowers and kissed her hand. Her movements were graceful and alluring as she allowed him to lead her on. He could hear the frantic pounding of her heart and noticed tears that glittered like jewels in her huge beautiful emerald eyes.

'Come my dear child, we must feed you now – I want you to be comfortable and happy here,' he said as he led her back inside the cottage.

She followed him as if in a dream; he led her into a small kitchen where he beckoned her to sit at the table upon which she saw several dishes of steaming hot food spread out.

'Take a seat and eat – you need to keep your strength up,' he told her.

'Serve her all that she needs,' he then instructed his manservant, who had stood back silently in the darkened room.

Claudette slowly walked over to the table and when she turned towards the door before sitting at the table, Dargo had gone.

Chapter Seventeen

Drasilla decided to pay a visit to Gilroy to ensure that both he and Bogey would keep out of sight when Errol arrived and on sweeping majestically into their quarters, as was her fashion, she discovered both Gilroy and Bogey fast asleep on their twin chaise lounges in front of the TV, snoring loudly almost in harmony with each other.

She now proceeded to look around their quarters but could see no sign of any suspicious activities. Surely if he had abducted Claudette, he would have to keep her in the vicinity of the dungeons. She nevertheless called out softly 'Claudette – are you here.'

But all she had heard was the rhythmic sound of Gilroy and Bogey snoring loudly. She stood there hands on hips – what were they both doing still sleeping this time of day when they should have been working.

She noted that a freshly ironed uniform for Gilroy was hanging up ready for him to go on his daily rounds inspecting all other security staff.

She now made her way down to the lowest part of the caves towards the dark and hidden dungeons. She was determined to see for herself if Gilroy had anything to hide.

Whilst walking along one of the dark corridors she heard a faint scratching sound; at first she thought it was probably one of the many small bats that frequented down in this part of her caves, but then she heard a whimpering sound; she stopped in her tracks and listened intently – it sounded like a young girl sobbing.

She called out, 'Is that you Claudette – where are you my dear?'

The sobbing continued and Drasilla walked very quickly passing each separate dungeon but there was no sign of a young girl crying. She began to run along the corridor calling out and then she heard a small shrill voice, quite clearly call out 'Yes, yes, it is I – please help me, please help me – I am here.'

She rushed forward anxious to get nearer, but in her haste she tripped and hit her head hard against the thick brick wall rendering her completely unconscious.

When Claude failed to find Madam in her office later, he proceeded to go looking for her. He knew that sometimes, as was her habit, she inspected all areas of her caves in spite of employing a Chief Security Inspector, namely Gilroy, for this particular task; the areas after all were vast and a great deal of time was put into making thorough inspections on a daily basis. She was very particular about the conditions of all the areas and most often wanted to see for herself.

Many of the other members of staff, particularly the tiny fairy maids were afraid to go down into the lower parts of the enormous cave as they were terrified of Gilroy.

Gilroy's reputation really did precede him and as much as he loved being cloaked in such an infamous and damaging image, which gave him an immense feeling of importance, he basically and foolishly dismissed the dangerous repercussions of such an evil persona, which after all was not his to feel proud of.

No matter how many times Bogey had begged him to turn himself in and try to convince the authorities that he was innocent of all crimes, he was really afraid that they would never believe him, as was the case of his place of origin where he had been banned for all time.

Meanwhile, Gilroy had just awoken from his sleep feeling extremely groggy almost as if he had been drugged, when he noticed Drasilla letting herself out of their quarters. He was mortified that it had been the one day that he had overslept. He quickly wrapped his dressing gown around himself and ran out after her along the corridors curious as to where she was going.

On catching up with Drasilla and seeing her collapsed form on the ground, he crouched anxiously over her near lifeless body, gently stroking one of her hands. When there was no sign of consciousness, he lifted her in his arms and began making his way back to his abode.

'Just a minute Gilroy, what have you done with Madam,' yelled Claude as he began ambling his way towards Gilroy.

Gilroy turned towards Claude looking distressed and somewhat guilty; it had become second nature to him throughout the years to show guilt even though he had been innocent whenever faced with accusations of vile acts.

'I, I, I just came upon Madam laying here unconscious,' he stuttered. I fear she tripped and fell hitting her head against the stone walling,' he added.

'Oh, you fear do you, a likely story Gilroy – you've been waiting for your chance to abduct Madam, like all the other poor defenseless victims that you have stored away in some God forsaken place,' Claude cried pointing one of his nobbly fingers at Gilroy.

'Oh, don't be so dramatic Claude, me old flower – you know that just isn't true; don't you know me by now – why, I would never do such a thing. It's true, I swear. I've just nearly tripped over her near lifeless body myself and I was just about to take her to my rooms while she recovered and I was going to call you.'

Just then Bogey came behind Claude and quickly held his arms behind him rendering him unable to move.

'You won't get away with this you two vile creatures. I will be sure to tell Sheriff Errol when he next comes here,' Claude said struggling and spitting within the tight hold of Bogey.

'Oh, that's just perfect Bogey,' Gilroy said looking completely deflated, 'Let him go right now; what on earth do you think you are doing. You are only making the situation worse and he is surely convinced now that we are planning to abduct Drasilla.'

Bogey immediately let go his grip on Claude and stood there looking embarrassed.

'Well, what was I supposed to do? I didn't know what to think when I saw you standing there with Drasilla all floppy in your arms and Claude getting his droopy drawers all in a twist as usual.'

'Alright, alright, let's get Drasilla back to her quarters and we need to call a doctor. Here you carry her Claude,' Gilroy said as he walked over to Claude, who suddenly stepped back suspicious of what Gilroy was going to do next.

'Oh for goodness sake you gruesome unsightly zombie – stop looking at me like that. I've done nothing but simply happen upon her and find her unconscious and the sooner we get some help for her, the better. Now take her and we will follow you.'

Claude stepped forward and took Drasilla in his arms securely and started back along the long dark corridor.

When he turned, Gilroy, pulling Bogey roughly by one arm, had quickly scuttled off in the opposite direction towards their own quarters.

'Where are you two going,' he called out but they did not respond. He rolled his eyes at the sight of the comedic pair scuttling away like scared rats. *They were certainly the most ridiculous creatures he had ever come across,* he thought to himself sniggering.

'But after all it had been easier than he had thought to fool them,' the dark figure chuckled as he walked calmly along the long corridors in the lower part of the caves with Drasilla hanging limply in his arms.

He hesitated for a second as he looked at the most beautiful face he had ever seen; Drasilla sighed in her deep sleep and her sooty black lashes fluttered for a second as if she was about to regain consciousness. He quickly continued along the corridor, her long full black gothic satin dress rustling and dragging on the ground as he carried her.

'Now I have the most powerful serum that I could possible wish for – the queen of the blue fairies,' he whispered to himself.

He began laughing loudly which echoed along the corridor causing all the small bats hanging around to lose their grip in fright and topple down all around.

Chapter Eighteen

'Quickly Bogey, let's get all our things together – we'll have to leave immediately. You know what this means,' Gilroy said breathlessly pushing Bogey and nearly knocking him over as they both flew through the door to their quarters.

'Take it easy will ya and no, I don't know what this means,' Bogey snarled as he regained his balance. He stood there looking at Gilroy, hands on his hips, clearly showing his indignation at Gilroy's irrational behavior.

'This is no time to act dumb Bogey, you know fine full well what this means. It means that we are going to be the number one suspects for the abduction of Claudette. I am the mighty Troll Warrior and I will be blamed for anything that Errol chooses to blame me for.'

'I don't understand, why should we be blamed for something that we have absolutely nothing to do with and what do you know about the disappearance of Claudette?' Bogey asked scratching his head.

'Because I am the Chief of Security and I know everything that goes on around here – now MOVE IT AND NOW,' Gilroy screamed at him.

They both flew around packing a small bag each, both silent now.

'And don't forget to pack my newly designed and fitted uniforms and be extra specially careful when packing them – I don't want them all creased up before I have even had a chance to wear them,' Gilroy said almost choking on his words at the realization that he was losing everything that he had worked for so hard.

'Yes, well, I hardly think you will be needing them now, so let's just travel light, shall we,' Bogey answered, always the sensible one in stressful circumstances.

After they had packed as much as they could, they began making their way through the dark long corridors to a secret opening exiting from the lower part of the caves.

When they arrived outside they both stood panting momentarily before making their way down the great winding pathway leading down to the surrounding forest around the gigantic rocky cave.

'Oh my God,' Bogey wailed, tears running down his face, 'I LOVED that cave with all my heart and felt so wanted for the first time in my life, we never had it so good; all the luxury we had ever dreamt of and all the food we could wish for. What are we going to do now; it's back to sleeping on damp moss for us now and back to baking and eating grasshoppers. I hate grasshoppers.'

'Oh pull yerself together will ya, ya great big cry baby. We've survived before sleeping on damp moss and eating grasshoppers. You used to love grasshopper sandwiches, especially with peanut butter spread over,' Gilroy said, now behaving as the levelheaded one of the team, desperately trying to placate him. He felt totally responsible for all the problems and danger they were forever being faced with. It was after all his problems and he hated having to drag Bogey down with him. He turned and hugged Bogey.

'I'm so sorry to put you through this time and time again my dear boy,' he said, huge tears rolling down his face again. 'I just can't seem to shake this ill-repute from my good name.'

'Well exactly, that's what I keep trying to tell you. You just have to face it once and for all and go turn yourself in.'

'No, Bogey, I can't do that. I would never see you again – I would lose you forever. Sheriff Errol would lock me up and throw away the key. In fact I think he would burn his own station down with me finally caught and detained inside.'

'Let's get going then and who is the cry baby now,' Bogey said as he put his arm around Gilroy's shoulder, his voice shaking with emotion.

'It's just you and me again Bogey, me old flower and let me tell you, I will be very happy going back to our old life being back on the road fancy free and eating grasshoppers again. What on earth have you got in that huge backpack,' he suddenly said as he turned Bogey around.

'Shush, be quiet,' Bogey whispered as he grasped at Gilroy's arm tightly holding him and then quickly pulling him down behind some bushes. 'I just heard some voices coming from further down. It sounds like Sheriff Errol and Dargo.'

They both lay down as they heard footsteps coming closer and closer their way.

'Not a sound Bogey,' whispered Gilroy. 'They must know about the secret doorway to the lower part of the caves otherwise they would not come this way. The Sheriff knows the normal entry route and if he wanted to go that way, they would certainly not be on foot, they would be driving through the main entry.'

Just then, through the bushes they could see the figures of Errol, Dargo and Gruntle emerging around the corner towards them.

Gilroy quickly clamped one hand over Bogey's mouth and one hand over his backside. Bogey very nearly spluttered as he knew that Gilroy was afraid that he would let off loud trumpets; he always let off loud trumpets when he was nervous.

'I know you find this amusing but don't make a sound,' Gilroy mouthed to Bogey. Bogey shook his head vigorously and closed his eyes praying that he would not lose control and giggle. Gilroy may let loose trumpets when he was nervous, but Bogey giggled uncontrollably in his nervousness.

As the three men came full into sight, they stopped right by the side of where Gilroy and Bogey were hiding. Gilroy had to use all his control to stop one of his trumpets erupting from his behind. He could not give them away by making such a loud sound. They would know for sure who was hiding before even catching sight of him.

'Nobody else knows about this secret doorway to the passage leading down to the dark lower part of the cave,' Errol said now to Dargo and Gruntle.

'Yes and if I know Drasilla, that is the only part of the caves that she would allow Gilroy to hide out in,' Dargo added.

'Well OK Gentlemen, let's go if you don't mind. The quicker we get there, the better. I just want to get my hands on that swine,' said Gruntle angrily.

'Let's go then; we'll waste no more time. As soon as we get inside, you go one way and I'll go the other Dargo. You come with me Sir,' Errol turned and said to Gruntle.

They quickly proceeded the same way that Gilroy and Bogey had come from.

Bogey let out a huge sigh of relief when they disappeared out of sight.

'That was a close shave; I thought we were going to be discovered for sure. I mean if Gruntle really does have second sight, he certainly did not show any signs of it just then; why I would almost be tempted to say that the old codger is a right con man.'

'Did you hear what he called me,' Gilroy suddenly said with indignation, his face so flushed that Bogey thought he was going to explode.

'Well, to be honest, I could hardly hear a thing with you nearly sitting on my face. What did he call you?' Bogey now asked.

'Why that old hairy wizardry crock called me a swine. How dare he call me a swine! That old relic has no right to go calling me such names.'

'Don't get your drawers in a flurry; why worry about a bit of name calling. I wouldn't care about being called a swine so why should you,' Bogey said sniggering.

'Yes, well, you are a swine,' Gilroy snarled angrily.

With that Gilroy stood up dragging Bogey with him. They both brushed themselves down and started off down the winding slope towards the surrounding woodland.

'Just so you know, I took it upon myself to pack as much food as I could in this backpack that you were just going to complain about when we were ready to leave the cave. Well at least when we get to our old haunt, we will have plenty of food and can have a feast this evening.'

'Oh goody, you old rascal you; I'm that proud of you,' Gilroy gushed as he caught Bogey in a crushing hug, kissing him repeatedly.

'Here, steady on, you're squashing all my goodies,' Bogey replied.

'What did you pack, tell me, tell me. I can't wait to tuck in to a feast,' Gilroy asked excitedly clutching at Bogey's throat nearly throttling him. No matter what situation they were in Gilroy could be relied upon to think of his stomach – nothing interfered with his appetite.

'All your favorites; we have chicken legs, meat pies, chicken and ham pies, cheese and pickles, scotch eggs, a selection of pastries and a couple of bottles of Drasilla's finest Champagne,' he said licking his lips and rubbing his hands together gleefully.

'Oh goody goody – I can't wait,' Gilroy said rubbing his fat hands together gleefully.

They were now getting closer and closer to their old hideaway haunt in the thickest part of the woodlands where the huge gnarled and overgrown trees and bushes completely sabotaged their hideaway and nobody could possibly find it.

When they were able to fight their way through the prickly thick shrubbery, they found the old battered wooden door in the old faithful great twisted tree. Its magic roots stretched far underground and deep into the woods, giving life to the other trees that in turn twisted and hugged each other to further enforce the secrecy of their hideaway.

They immediately heard their neighbours, the bat mice who had also found solace amongst the great twisted branches.

As if able to sniff out food, especially cheese, Alfred, the oldest bat mouse called out to Gilroy.

'Hey Gilroy, where have you been and what's that smell; I can smell the most sumptuous cheese; could you spare some for your old friends.'

'If you must know Alfred, we've been on holiday in the South of France sunning ourselves and living it up with the rich and famous. And, yes we do have some really creamy cheese; if you could just give us a few minutes to get ourselves ensconced back in our very humble abode, we can give you some,' Gilroy said sighing.

'You just can't help embellishing your life, can you,' Bogey said rolling his eyes. 'In the South of France indeed – you wished.'

'Home sweet home – give him some of that cheese for God's sake, otherwise he will be bugging the life out of us,' Gilroy then turned to Bogey, his eyes rolling ignoring his remark.

'Well, I tell you what,' Alfred now said, 'my little beauty of a wife Priscilla is preparing my supper and we are having ham, eggs and chips with doorstep slices of bread and you are both invited as a welcoming back gesture.'

'Ooooh I love you – that is so good of you Alfred,' Bogey told him. 'We would love to and you are most welcome to have some of our cheese. In fact we have a good bottle of wine to go with.'

As much as they had dreaded returning to their old haunt they now felt so much better and the thought of sitting in Priscilla's lovely warm parlor and having a good hearty comforting meal made them feel all warm inside. They hurriedly unpacked their few belongings and then presented themselves at Priscilla's door.

'I told you Bogey, didn't I that we would soon get back into our old life,' Gilroy said winking at Bogey.

Chapter Nineteen

Errol, Dargo and Gruntle finally reached the secret door leading to the lower part of the cave. As suggested by Errol, Dargo went one way and Errol and Gruntle went the other way in search of Gilroy and Bogey.

After thoroughly searching all the dungeons in the lower part of the cave and finding no sign of Gilroy and Bogey, they decided to go to the upper levels where they quickly came upon Claude tied up with thick rope grunting and groaning. When he caught sight of them he began struggling frantically.

'Not again Claude, this is becoming a habit with you,' Errol said as he knelt down on one knee to rip the tape off from around his mouth. 'What is going on here and where are your clothes?' he then asked, noticing that Claude was all down to his vest and long thermal under pants.

'Oh thank you kindly Sir,' Claude spluttered in pure relief when the tape was removed from his mouth. 'I'm afraid that Madam has been abducted and I was rendered helpless to stop it.'

'Now you can't blame that on me,' Dargo readily quipped.

'Hah, a fine body guard you are. Why were you not here guarding her?' Gruntle asked spluttering, his face going a deep purple.

'I can't be in two places at once can I?' Dargo replied angrily.

'Tell us what happened,' Errol now asked, ignoring both Gruntle and Dargo.

'I can only think it was Gilroy Sir, he must have come up behind me and hit me over the head and when I fell to the ground unconscious, he then must have quickly tied me up and taped my mouth.'

'Just a minute Claude – I mean do you know how ridiculous that sounds – you can only think... he must have come up behind you and hit you over the head and then must have tied you up,' Errol said sighing deeply as he turned to both Dargo and Gruntle.

'Either you saw him and know that he did this to you – or, you didn't,' he added clicking his tongue. This was a well known habit of his when he was near to losing all his patience.

'Well, I smelt him and there is no other smell like it,' Claude replied.

'Oh, I see you smelt him,' Errol snorted rolling his eyes.

'One thing for sure is that I am almost certain that I heard a young girl sobbing in the lower part of the caves earlier this day,' Claude added.

Gruntle suddenly went a deeper shade of purple and turned on his heels quickly to make his way back down to the lower part of the cave but Dargo made a grab for him and held him back, holding onto to his arms tightly.

Gruntle struggled and angrily shook himself free of Dargo's grasp giving him such a black look that for a second Dargo thought he was going to throw a punch at him.

'I will cast a spell on him and make him into the ugliest little toad you could ever imagine, even uglier than he already is,' Gruntle said through gritted teeth, 'And, then I will stomp on him squashing him until he is completely flattened and then feed him to the birds.'

'Calm down, I don't even think the birds would have any appetite for Gilroy,' Dargo told him. 'Yes, yes, I know this is no laughing matter,' he hastily added as he saw Gruntle's expression of frustration and sheer rage. 'We must keep our wits about us and think clearly. The only place Gilroy could go back to is his old haunt in the thick of the woods. I've tried many times to track him down but I've never been able to find his hideout.'

'Then we will search the whole area night and day until we find him and we won't give up until we do,' Errol now told them. 'This has gone on far too long and we must apprehend him once and for all and I'm telling you that when I get hold of him, I'm going to lock him up and throw away the key.'

'Excuse me Sirs, could I ask you to kindly just untie me before you go. My hands have gone numb from the tightness of the ropes. Also, I've not had my breakfast and I am famished. Could I interest you gentlemen to join me before you go off searching for Gilroy?'

'No thanks Claude, but we will come through to the kitchen and talk to some of the staff you work with; maybe one of the other members of staff saw something suspicious going on earlier,' Errol replied.

'I would also like to take a look around Drasilla's apartment to see if there are any signs of anything suspicious before she was taken,' Dargo said.

'What exactly were you doing in the lower part of the cave anyway; I wouldn't have thought that anyone occupied this part of the caves?' Errol now asked Claude frowning.

'Well, Madam had called me earlier to question me about the past evening as she was of the opinion that something amiss had gone on during the evening resulting in your inebriated condition Sir. We were at that time interrupted by a telephone call so she asked me to return back later, which I did. When I could not find her, I then came down here to see if she was conducting one of her inspections, as she sometimes does. The next thing, I felt a blow to my head and I could see stars in front of my eyes.'

'Why are you so convinced that Gilroy had anything to do with this?' asked Dargo looking very somber. 'And, how would he have gained access to the lower parts of the cave?'

'Sir, believe me, as I mentioned before, there is no mistaking the smell of Gilroy. I mean that smell gives him away even before you see him,' Claude answered emphatically.

'But, you never actually saw him?' Errol then asked again.

After untying the rope from Claude, they followed him back to the kitchen and while he ate his breakfast they questioned all the other members of staff who insisted that they had not seen anything suspicious earlier. In fact, they all made it quite clear that they had very little to do with Gilroy and Bogey and that the only person who saw Gilroy and Bogey on a regular basis from day to day was Claude and of course Madam.

'But wait a minute, I've just remembered something,' Mason, the chauffer now offered up. 'I thought it a bit strange at the time but really didn't think much about it after. I had gone off looking for Wally earlier today, he does like to roam around the caves sometimes and I came across Wally growling at Gilroy loitering outside and Gilroy started to throw rocks at him. I shouted at Gilroy to put the rocks down and he just ran off.'

'What's so strange about that, it sounds like Wally is a very good guard dog,' replied Errol.

'Well, because Wally loves Gilroy and he often goes down to their part of the cave to sit with them. In fact Gilroy and Bogey frequently takes him out walking around the caves. Wally of course is quite partial to having tit bits from them of course and they are always throwing chicken bones and little bits of steak his way when he goes down. Like all dogs he knows where he can get leftover food from.'

'Well, we have now been able to establish categorically that Gilroy and Bogey do reside here,' Errol declared now looking accusingly at Claude. 'And of course he would have access to the lower part of the cave and would know of the secret opening/exit. Did you see Gilroy after that?' he asked turning back from the window, now looking at Mason intently.

'Yes, I followed Wally down to their quarters shortly after and asked Gilroy about the incident earlier but he looked puzzled and said that he would never throw stones at Wally. Wally of course ran to him as usual wagging his tail and Gilroy as usual rolled on the floor with him tickling him as he always does. Both Gilroy and Bogey love him.'

'Now I have an idea Mason and with your permission I would like to borrow Wally as I think he would be invaluable for our search for Gilroy,' Errol said.

Mason looked concerned and averted his eyes downcast. Wally immediately came to him pushing his nose against one of his legs whining. He could sense Mason's anxiety and then stood up on his hind legs scratching away at Mason's legs.

'What is it boy?' Mason said as he fondled his head affectionately.

'I'm not sure that I could let you do that Sheriff. Apart from anything else, if he did lead you to Gilroy and you then apprehended him, Wally would sense that you were harming Gilroy and he may well attack you.'

Errol immediately stepped over to the side of Mason and started petting Wally, stroking the back of his head and playfully tugging at his ears. Wally sat there wagging his tail and panting in his enjoyment of the attention. When Errol offered out his hand in front of Wally's mouth, Wally started licking it as if accepting Errol as a new found dear friend.

'There now Wally, are you willing to help me find Gilroy, we need to question him and we need your valuable help.'

Wally stood up on his hind legs barking as if acknowledging the important task he was being asked to undertake. Wagging his tail he then held out one paw which Errol took hold of and shook.

'Good boy, good boy, I knew I could count on you – that's a deal then,' Errol said pleased with himself as he turned smiling at the group around him.

Mason stood back with a look of apprehension on his face as he beckoned Wally back at his side.

'I'm not sure about this,' he muttered under his breath. I don't like the idea of Wally tracking Gilroy down like he was some kind of dangerous predator. I know he smells and appears to be quite an unsavory character but I believe that he is a good person underneath that snarling guise he thinks he should present just to appear important, no matter how dangerous it is to himself. I think he is just a comical but hideous looking Troll who just craves affection where he can get it, which I do really think is an endearing quality in some way, don't ask me to explain that; I just have that feeling whenever I am around him.'

'Yes, well Mason, that sounds all very sentimental to me but I don't think you fully understand the seriousness of this; he is most definitely and without doubt a very dangerous predator and has been for many years.'

'Dogs sense an unkind cruel person and their lips immediately curl up into a snarl whenever they come up against such a person. Where Gilroy is concerned Wally runs to him wagging his tail and they spend hours out walking together and Gilroy is always very playful with him.'

'Oh my God,' Gruntle now growled. 'Are we going to stand around here discussing how loveable Gilroy really is? I'm telling you, I don't believe a word of it; he is nothing but an evil Troll and we need to get on our way to find him and my precious little Claudette.'

'And Drasilla, don't forget Drasilla,' Dargo then said, looking deep in thought; he had been very quiet throughout the questioning of the staff.

'Right then, let's get going,' Errol stood up briskly. 'And as for you Claude, you are coming with us. You have kept important information from us and I am going to detain you in one of my cells for further questioning.'

Chapter Twenty

The pounding on the heavy wooden door penetrated through the deep layers of her sleep. Drasilla desperately fought the thick mist forcing her eyes closed, making her body heavy and listless; it was as if she had been drugged. When she was able to force her aching eyelids open, she could see sunlight streaming through the huge bedchamber. She had no idea how long she had slept; she sat up slowly and looked around the huge dark looming bedchamber.

The pounding on the door began again, this time more desperately; the sound echoed in her head, thundered at her temples. She rubbed her temples in an attempt to relieve the pain pounding in her head. Dragging herself up from the bed, she moved slowly towards the door. Her hand trembled as she opened the door.

Dargo stood in the hallway like a lofty dark sinister shadow hovering over her at the doorway, a sardonic cruel grin curling his lips; his dark eyes moved possessively over her face. Her breath caught in her throat as he lowered his head inches from hers so that she could feel the warmth of his breath on her skin.

His eyes were like blazing torches and Drasilla trembled like a bird beneath their influence and could not remove her gaze from them. Her heart was pounding as he leaned forward and took hold of her trembling body in his arms. She pushed against his massive chest, struggling to free herself from his strong grasp. He tightened his hold, amusement spreading over his face. She tried not to let her fear show on her face although she visibly shuddered.

She broke from his embrace as he set her down and ran across the room as far away from him as she could, forcing herself to remain calm but her emotions were running out of control and she slumped on the bed, all strength draining out of her.

Dargo suddenly inhaled sharply, uttering a terrible gagging sound, strained and full of anguish. He threw himself by the side of the bed and crouched at her side, weeping loudly. She was overwhelmed with emotion as she looked down at his face; the tears glistening in his eyes as he gazed back at her. Those eyes could mesmerize and hypnotize, rendering a person spellbound, just like the power of his voice. She stretched over and stroked his brow feeling an overpowering feeling of tenderness seeing him so full of sorrow.

'What is it Dargo – you know you can tell me anything. Whatever is happening to you, I will understand and not judge you – we can help you. Let me help you,' she implored him still stroking his brow tenderly. She could not bear to see him weeping like this.

A curious hush fell in the room as he suddenly sprang back up from the floor, threw his head back and began roaring with laughter, taunting her with his eyes, savage brutal joy spreading over his chiselled features.

He had a hard arrogance, an air of complete command and she suddenly realized that she was in the presence of a very evil person. He gathered her roughly into his arms, imprisoning her against his mighty chest, whirled around and carried her from the chamber room, his face set like a granite mask as he marched along the hallway. Her heart was beating out of control. Her whole body tensed up as she pushed against his shoulders, struggling uselessly.

'Welcome to my home,' he said as he slowly but reluctantly set her down allowing her feet to touch the threshold of a massive dark drawing room.

Drasilla stood there looking at Dargo furious beyond words, suddenly forgetting all her fear and feelings of foreboding; her mind had suddenly cleared as if a thick fog had lifted from around her; she felt all sensible rational thought, common sense and calm return and was able to think clearly. It was after all only Dargo, whom she had known for as long as she could remember.

There must be some rational explanation for his bizarre behaviour and I must not let him feel that I am afraid of him. He will come to his senses if I just act calm, she thought to herself. She decided to try her usual diva demeanour on him; it always amused him.

To be held against her will was bad enough, but to be without all her necessary cosmetics and beautiful gowns was unforgiveable. The idea that he had dragged her away from her place of great taste and elegance to this huge manly cold fortress, which as far as she could see had no hint of warmth or elegant furnishing, was unacceptable.

Dargo stood grinning at her, his handsome face had ordinarily never failed to cause Drasilla to sigh in appreciation of such beauty, but now she felt no such appreciation.

'What is the meaning of this Dargo? I am completely baffled by your motive. You simply cannot hold me here against my will; I have work to do and will not tolerate this stupidity. Not only is it inconvenient to me but most exasperating and completely out of your good nature to do such a thing.'

Dargo threw back his head and roared with laughter again.

'And you Madam are most exquisite and charming when you are angry.'

Drasilla again detected a hint of cruelty in the unpleasant curl of Dargo's lips as he smiled, totally unfamiliar to his character and she felt her whole body shuddering again with fear.

'Is this some kind of joke you are playing on me Dargo. This is so out of character of you to do something like this. Take me back immediately or I will have no other choice but to phone Errol.'

Dargo laughed again as he suddenly produced her pink mobile phone encrusted with tiny diamonds which glittered in his hand. It was well known that Drasilla loved diamonds and most everything was encrusted with diamonds. Her jewellery was impressive and apart from the usual colossal collection of trinkets including necklaces, bracelets, rings and earrings, several of her gowns were encrusted with diamonds.

Drasilla gasped as she now saw her mobile in Dargo's huge hand but she could see that there was no point in becoming angry so she instead decided to become flirtatious with him and try to find out what exactly he was planning to do with her.

'Why Dargo, I do believe you have abducted me to get back at Errol. I had every intention of inviting you over to join us for dinner but I think you would have been bored with Errol's talk about me harbouring dangerous criminals in my caves.'

'You flatter yourself Madam, but, talking about harbouring dangerous criminals, Errol has every intention of searching out Gilroy. Needless to say that Gilroy wasted no time and scarpered from your premises as quickly as he could but both the Sheriff and Gruntle are hot on his trail this very minute with the help of Mason's devoted dog who they have every confidence in to sniff out Gilroy very quickly. They really believe that he will not get away this time,' Dargo replied mockingly.

Drasilla sat there studying Dargo's face and expressions; she had never seen him like this. They had all wondered if sooner or later he would perhaps falter under all the pressure he had gone through after the disappearance of his wife and daughter but time had gone on and he had seemed to have just got stronger and more determined to find them.

'Why are you doing this Dargo?' she now asked him again. 'I do understand how much you have gone through and I have been proud of you at the way you've handle yourself. In fact everybody has watched how you have remained so strong throughout the whole ordeal apart from the odd binge with your tipple that you have taken to. What has finally tipped you over the edge to now do such a thing?'

'It is quite simple my dear girl. I lost my wife and daughter and now I have decided to replace them with you as my wife and Claudette as my daughter and together we will make a delightful family, don't you agree?'

'Oh my God, Dargo you can't do this.'

'Oh but I have my darling girl,' Dargo said grinning menacingly. His whole expression was now that of a mad man; his eyes had suddenly gone black and his lips took on an evil cruel twist.

'So it is you that abducted Claudette just as Gruntle suspected. Where is Claudette now – I hope you have not harmed her in any way Dargo.'

'She is unharmed and sleeping very peacefully this very moment in my cottage in the very darkest and deepest part of the forest land. Apart from her hair turning completely white, she is quite safe so don't worry my darling girl. I plan to bring her here so that the two of you can bond as a family.

'Why on earth would you take her to your cottage in the woodlands, so near to Gruntle and Errol?'

'Where else would I keep her my darling girl – it was nearby and convenient for me at the time,' Dargo replied.

'So why did you bring me here?' Drasilla asked him.

'Because this is my fortress my darling girl and I have much work to do in my laboratory – but, don't worry, as I have just told you I am planning to bring Claudette here.

'Will you stop calling me your darling girl; I am not your darling girl Dargo. What on earth do you plan to do with us in your laboratory? Have you gone stark staring mad? I beg you to turn yourself in and release myself and Claudette immediately.'

'You know I am not going to do that Drasilla. As I've just told you, that old addled minded Wizard and Errol are looking for Gilroy, the mighty Troll Warrior, as the chief suspect and if I know Gilroy, as comical and dumb as he acts and I give him full credit for that, he will outsmart them every time. In their sheer determination to find him, and you know how vain they both are; they will refuse to admit that he has outsmarted them every time. They will go on and on regardless in their relentless search for him, while all the time forgetting about the purpose of their search. You and Claudette will just fade in their minds – they will be so engrossed in capturing Gilroy.

As you know, Errol is so full of his own self importance and has to prove himself as a conscientious persevering Sheriff; the whole object of his industrious line of thought is catching Gilroy, whilst forgetting exactly why he needs to catch him. And, of course the victims namely you and Claudette will be sadly forgotten in the process as I have said. Gilroy has been on the run for many years and they are not about to catch him now even with a stupid dog sniffing him out.'

With that said Dargo turned and started to stride out of the room but before going out of the huge cold chamber, he halted at the doorway and suddenly strode back over to Drasilla who just as suddenly drew back from him as he came closer to her. Dargo bent over, placed his huge hands around her tiny waist, lifted her into the air and roughly kissed her full on the lips.

Drasilla gasped and quickly slapped him around his face. She shuddered all over furious that he had the nerve to actually do that to her.

'That is no way to treat your husband when he kisses you goodbye. But I hope you will appreciate that I am going to collect some of your gowns, cosmetics and toiletries, as requested my lady, so you should treat me well,' he said now releasing her and bowing graciously, mocking her indignation.

'How dare you touch me, I will not be man handled like that and I trust you not to ever do that again,' she said spluttering with sheer rage at his rough handling of her.

'There is a bell cord over there, just ring when you feel you are ready to have breakfast. I've a very loyal man servant who is only happy to serve you whatever you want. Feel free to take a shower when you want. I will not be too long my dear.'

Dargo again strode over to the huge wooden door, paused and held out a huge key which he dangled into the air to torment her contemptuously before closing the door behind him and locking it loudly and securely.

She could hear him laughing loudly and his loud clomping footsteps advancing along the corridor. She turned and ran to the window but halted completely deflated as she now saw wrought iron bars across. She grasped at the iron bars rattling them loudly when she suddenly saw a large bent figure walking outside. She called out but the figure just kept walking without turning towards the window. She pressed herself up against the iron bars straining to see the figure more clearly.

'Why that is Gilroy,' she whispered to herself. 'What is he doing here; surely he would not come here knowing that they are looking for him.' *Or, maybe he knew that Dargo had bought her here and had come to rescue her,* she now pondered feeling a little more optimistic.

She turned away from the window frantically looking for something to throw at the window to alert his attention to her. She took hold of one heavy brass candle holder and threw it at the window as hard as she could; it clattered loudly against the wrought iron bars but the bent figure, after enveloping himself in his cloak retreated behind a stone statue and was lost to view. As he disappeared, a moaning wind began to build up and heavy rain descended which hammered against the window until her view was completely obstructed.

Drasilla had always been a woman of immense good common sense and she now decided to stay completely calm. She would first ring for breakfast; after all she was starving and needed to keep up her strength. She would then take a long hot shower before Dargo's return and then later try to reason with him again.

In the meantime she also planned to question the man servant and find out exactly where Claudette was being kept. She needed to talk to the girl and find out how she was coping in the situation. One thing was sure though, was that she was quite certain and confident that Dargo obviously had no intention of harming either one of them.

She walked over to the bell cord and pulled it vigorously. A few minutes later she heard the door being unlocked and in walked the manservant who immediately bowed to her.

'How may I help you Madam?' the man servant now asked her.

'Claude, what on earth are you doing here?' Drasilla asked as she drew in her breath startled to see him. You must help me immediately to find Claudette and then take me back to my cave.'

'You are mistaken Madam; I'm not Claude – I am his twin brother and my name is Baldric. We parted on not so friendly terms and have not seen each other for years. Now, if you would be so kind as to let me know what you would like for breakfast I can serve you as quickly as possible and be on my way about my other tasks. The Master will return very soon and I must complete my tasks before his return.'

'But Baldric I can help you reconcile with Claude; he works for me and if you wanted we could do that right now. He is a good man and I'm sure he would be so happy to see you.'

'Has he even ever mentioned that he has a twin brother Madam – has he ever talked about me at all?' Baldric asked his eyes welling up with gooey greenish tears.

'No, but Claude says very little anyway and of course would never discuss any personal matters with me; he is just not the type to even complain about anything or bare his heart to anybody.'

'I don't wish to be rude Madam but I really do need to get on with my duties before the Master returns.'

Drasilla stood looking at him intently before instructing him what she would like for her breakfast.

'Well then my good man I would like porridge with strawberries, strong hot black coffee and some Danish pastries,' she replied very calmly.

'Very well Madam,' Baldric said bowing as he turned and left. She heard him lock the door securely from the outside.

'That is so incredible – the likeness is uncanny right down to the same greenish goofy teeth – my God, two of them,' she muttered to herself.

Chapter Twenty-One

Gilroy ambled to the door proudly wearing his flamboyant flowered pinafore and nothing much else on hearing a loud urgent hammering sound; the pinafore had been a gift from Bogey in celebration of returning to their old abode following their flight from the cave.

It was his turn to cook dinner and he was in the middle of preparing an exceptionally hot chicken curry, a dish which both he and bogey enjoyed immensely. Both would suffer after the meal as usually a hot curry would have a disastrous effect on Gilroy's stomach and an equally disastrous effect on Bogey's delicate sense of smell.

'See that we have plenty of ginger beer on the table,' he yelled out to Bogey as he opened the door wielding a wooden kitchen utensil that he had been using to stir the thick curry sauce.

He stood looking at the person on his doorstep with his mouth wide open, his heart hammering so loudly that he could actually feel it nearly jumping out of his chest. He leaned forward slightly and looked from left to right before rudely grabbing the visitor by the scruff of his neck and literally dragging him inside.

'What are you doing coming here like this, did anyone follow you?' he said while quickly snatching the huge basket of food being held out towards him and clutching it closely to his chest as if afraid that it was going to be immediately snatched back from his firm grasp.

'Quickly, take this into the kitchen,' he called out to Bogey. As usual when he became excited, he began to pass loud outbursts of wind, almost of a melodic and constant rhythm of loud noises; melodic gems as he usually called them with immense pride, but certainly not a pleasing or interesting tone to the ear or particularly agreeable to any other sense or taste.

Bogey then came rushing through to their lounge clutching cans of ginger beer in his arms and on seeing their visitor, he stopped dead in his tracks dropping all the cans onto the floor where they then rolled across to where Gilroy was standing causing him to lose his balance and topple over backwards. He lay sprawled on his back, legs splayed out in the air and his face beginning to redden with sheer rage. Bright lights flashed before his eyes as he lay immobile for a few seconds, staring at the ceiling, gasping for breath before he roared out loud in fury.

'You imbecile,' Gilroy spat out almost choking in his exasperation at Bogey's clumsiness. 'I am fed up with your total incompetence to do anything without causing injury to me; you great lumbering, uncouth gawky hog.'

'What on earth are you doing here Claude, are you mad. You know you shouldn't come to this part of the woods. What if someone followed you?' Bogey said completely ignoring Gilroy, refusing to pay any attention to his constant futile verbal abuse and name calling. He could at times be most ill-tempered, grouchy, and peevish beyond understanding and belief.

Claude stood there looking at them both, panting and puffing. He looked extremely agitated and disturbed. Neither Gilroy nor Bogey had ever seen him looking so distraught; even his usually greasy slicked back hair was all askew, giving him the appearance of a slightly wacky, unrestrained and out of control nutty professor. His usually smart appearance was also in complete disarray. In fact he looked to be a man in total chaos.

'I just felt I had to come here to warn you that the Sheriff has sought to obtain the assistance of Mason's dog Wally to track you down. I've just spent a whole day and night in a cell with the Sheriff questioning me relentlessly about your movements and whereabouts. When I left the station I went straight back to Madam's cave through the secret tunnel; I was being followed initially but the poor man could not keep up with me. I loaded up the food basket as I was worried that you would not have anything to eat although I should have known better.'

'But mores to the point,' Bogey suddenly interrupted scratching his head, 'why do they want to know about your movements Gilroy. They know full well that you have a dodgy stomach and have been plagued with intestinal gas causing you to constantly pass wind. Why belching, bloating, flatulence and farting is part of your daily life and everybody knows that; it might be a bit embarrassing but no secret to anyone within a radius of a couple of miles from one of your explosive outbursts.'

Gilroy suddenly sprang up from the floor, the basket having already toppled to one side when he fell and he began chasing Bogey around the room waving the wooden spoon menacingly. Bogey ducked and dived behind the dining table and chairs before hitting his big toe on one of the chairs causing him to roll over onto the floor in agony.

'Don't make me come over there and whack you around the head,' Gilroy said spluttering, his eyes rolling. 'Just zip it will ya and listen to what Claude is trying to tell us.'

'Oooh my toe; look it's beginning to go blue,' Bogey whined in abstract pain, trying to suck his own toe.

'I'll give you blue toe, I'll give you something to really cry about if I come over there and batter you about your head and then you will be black and blue all over,' Gilroy retorted before he flopped down onto the nearest chair in sheer exhaustion.

'You give me heart palpitations with your idiocy. I wonder sometimes at your complete lack of common sense and I am just at a loss for words, I don't think you have a single brain cell in your fuzzy head and I despair of you,' he continued as he flung the wooden spoon dramatically to the floor. 'But anyway Claude, take no notice of him and continue with what you were saying before being rudely interrupted by dopey here.'

'Yes, Claude just ignore the name calling; it's just a part of my daily vocabulary education,' Bogey said poking his tongue out at Gilroy.

Claude looked from one to the other and suddenly burst out laughing. They never failed to amuse him with their antics. Both Gilroy and Bogey stared at him as if he had finally lost his marbles. He had missed them both immensely and seeing them in all their crude absurdity made him feel a huge rush of affection for them. He strode over to Gilroy and hugged him before beckoning Bogey to join in a threesome hug.

All three of them burst into tears in synchronization. The strain of their situation had finally got the better of them, but it was a relief to let loose their emotions although the outpourings of a slimy green substance rushing from Claude's nose immediately halted their threesome hug as they quickly stepped back from him. Gilroy pulled off his pinafore and handed it to Claude to wipe his nose much to the disapproval of Bogey.

'Hey that's my gift to you and you go and give it to Claude to wipe his green snot on,' he said, but thought better of saying anything further when seeing the way Gilroy was looking at him as he proceeded to pick up the wooden spoon again and shake it at him as a silent warning.

'Well anyway Claude,' Gilroy now told him as he linked his arm fondly through his. 'You've to join us for dinner my friend, I insist but first go take a shower and freshen yourself up; you look absolutely frightful,' he added winking at Bogey.

Trembling with happiness, Claude thanked him as he handed back the pinafore. Gilroy controlled his facial expression as he carefully took back the soiled pinafore with the lips of two of his fingers, attempting to stifle his gagging all the while much to Bogey's amusement.

'I've a better idea,' Claude answered smiling. 'I will finish the meal and serve it up to you like old times – I insist.'

'Well, if you insist, let's drink to that – open three cans of ginger beer my own dear boy,' Gilroy said slapping Bogey on his back playfully and planting a big kiss on his cheek. 'We can have a little celebration today and have a feast.'

Bogey danced into the kitchen with the luxury gourmet food hamper which contained all their favourite foods including cold meats and pies, chicken legs, a variety of cheeses and bread, quiche, fruit cakes, jams and pickles and of course champagne, ginger beer and ale.

They raised their glasses and vowed to remain friends forever. Gilroy was blissfully contented as they stood slurping down the beer. They had now become like three musketeers in their union together. His heart was nearly bursting with happiness and tears of pure joy rolled down his face.

'Oh he's off again,' Bogey said laughing.

'Oh you two; one minute you are nigh on nearly killing each other and the next you are sobbing and professing undying eternal love for each other.'

'Yes, well you wouldn't understand really Claude,' Gilroy said as he wrapped his arms around Bogey's neck nearly choking him. 'You see over the years, we have become inseparable and we are many things to each other. I would do anything for Bogey and he would do anything for me and the chain of trust between the two of us is unbreakable. You see we are more than just friends, we are like brothers and so you wouldn't really understand how that feels.'

A look of sheer sadness seemed to wash over Claude's face as he turned and walked towards their bathroom.

'I suppose you are right of course,' they heard him mutter as he went into the bathroom before closing the door.

After Claude had showered, he went straight into the kitchen, finished cooking the meal and then proudly served them at the table. When he sat down at the table to eat with them he felt a rush of both sadness and happiness; he was sad that they were all in danger but happy that they were united together as friends who would forever protect each other without any qualms.

The meal was delicious and they ate every morsel with total enjoyment as Claude was an extremely proficient cook. Although Madam knew of his culinary skills she was reluctant to allow him to touch any food in the kitchen which wounded his feelings immensely. He couldn't understand what she had against him touching and preparing food for her but he had been just as happy to serve her in any other way that he could.

'That was a magnificent meal,' Gilroy said with enormous gusto burping in his appreciation. 'I tell you, I've missed you serving us Claude, but my friend you know you can stay here as long as you want and we will be strong together.'

They raised their glasses again as they stood up from the table and staggered, hardly able to move, their stomachs fit to burst, into the drawing room ready to recline onto plump comfortable easy chairs.

'This is the life – we are princes together. The Three Buccaneers,' Bogey said swaying on his feet grinning from ear to ear at Claude and Gilroy who just as drunkenly swayed from side to side.

Claude nevertheless, regardless of his drunken state and blurred vision, looked around the drawing room in utter astonishment. He had not noticed on first arriving but now saw that all the luxurious furnishings from their quarters in the cave had been transferred over to their secret abode tucked away in the woodlands. He raised an eyebrow, puzzled now at their extraordinary skill of siphoning and transferring all their personal effects with such speed and ease. From the outside their small humble cottage looked far too small for such a large amount of furniture but the inside of their cottage was surprisingly spacious.

'Oh don't worry Claude,' Gilroy said immediately sensing his bewilderment. 'We have been collecting our things during the past few nights with the help of the three Pug brothers, Clancy, Cedric and Cecil, who have been of a great assistance to us. They know of all the secret passageways in the cave, some of them we did not even know of ourselves. I know what you are thinking, can we trust them and I can tell you that we can; like us they are misfits amongst even their own clan – we can find a lot of little tasks for them to do in exchange for some of our food. We also helped ourselves to food from the expansive food storage pantry area in Madam's kitchen. After all, you would not expect us to starve, would you,' he said laughing.

'I certainly would not,' Claude answered laughing as they both looked at each other, their eyes rolling on seeing Bogey at this instant fast asleep snoring loudly.

'That dear boy,' Gilroy now said. 'He is my soul mate and I love him like my own son; my life would be nothing without him.'

'Yes alright Gilroy, we have heard more than enough of your declarations of love this evening,' muttered Bogey with one eye half open.

He can't take his drink very well,' Gilroy continued to a sleepy Claude, who could only now also look at him with one eye open.

'Mind you, he has been very busy these past couple of days running around arranging all our belongings. We were sorry to leave the cave and became used to Madam's luxurious surroundings and we felt that a certain amount of the class rubbed off on us.'

'Yes, quite,' Claude murmured with a half grin on his face as he lowered himself onto one of their plump and comfortable sofas. He was dead on his legs and needed to rest.

As soon as Claude's eyes closed and his breathing became steady indicating that he was fast asleep, Gilroy quickly went to their side door to let in the three Pug brothers, Clancy, Cedric and Cecil who in turn tiptoed inside towards the kitchen. Together they quickly and quietly as they could, cleared all plates and dishes used while Gilroy prepared a spread of sandwiches, pies, chicken legs and lemonade squash for them.

'Ooh you Darling you,' Clancy gushed as he rushed forward to embrace Gilroy. 'I just adore you as ugly as you are, I want to hug and kiss you. You are like the fairy godmother, the ugly sister and beauty and the beast all rolled into one.'

'Shush – less of your cheek, never mind about that, just be quiet and when you have finished eating, please clear up after you. I want to see clean dishes and a cleared and orderly kitchen tomorrow morning.'

'Oh my, you have become house proud sweetie pie,' Clancy said as he minced and strutted his stuff in his newly acquired sequinned high heeled shoes around the kitchen.

'Well my dears, don't just stand there with your gaping mouths, let's tuck in; we don't get treated like princes often do we – let's enjoy it,' he told Cedric and Cecil, rubbing his hands together gleefully.

Gilroy quietly closed the door to the dining room as he silently crept back to the sitting room and joined Bogey on one of the sofas.

Before long all three were slumped fast asleep snoring loudly; Bogey and Gilroy had legs and arms entwined about each other with a smile of pure contentment on their faces; Claude was half draped on the sofa, his long misshapen legs and arms dangling over the side. For now they were safe; they had feasted on good food and were warm and cosy.

But they were oblivious to a sinister face peering through the window at them; a face filled with abhorrence and destruction. The face disappeared as quickly as it had appeared but it was plain that their hideout was not as secure as they believed it to be.

A storm had developed and the great gnarled trees outside swayed and rattled against their windows forebodingly but still they did not awaken; they were oblivious of the impending danger before long about to befall upon them.

Chapter Twenty-Two

Dargo stood admiring the vast beautiful and enduring countryside from outside his small cottage in the deepest and darkest part of the forest. He inhaled deeply, closing his mind to all his misgivings, attempting to tuck them deep down within his very heart and soul.

He could no longer fool himself and slowly with infinite weariness, he decided with determined finality to end his utter and total anguish. He promised himself that he would endeavour to thrust away the stark, raw loneliness of his existence and felt an immense sense of peace within himself this morning.

The darkness within him had grown to overwhelming proportions and had spread in him until every fibre of his body had been frozen of all emotion. Grief had besieged his mind, consumed him until his heart and soul had roared out his pain like the wounded animal that he had allowed himself to become. He would cast away all these demons and endeavour to replace darkness with light.

He could no longer bear to be alone and he promised himself this day to embrace everything and anything that provided solace for his mind and soul. He needed to find something or somebody to calm the raging demons inside his mind. He had been burning with rage for too long and had been consumed with it. He made up his mind to slowly unravel himself from the darkness that he had created to exist in.

He turned abruptly and strode back into his small cottage determined to forge ahead with a fresh outlook on life. He would go out today into the deepest part of the forest and find The Troll Warrior with or without Errol even if it meant exposing himself to the very jaws of danger.

But then he had been living for too long in the midst of danger on a daily basis; it seemed he had to be always fighting for normal existence, forever searching for his family and battling with the Troll Warrior – but that would end soon and he wanted it to end today.

He knew what he needed to do now and he began preparing himself for a final battle with the Troll Warrior. He needed, more than anything, to settle things once and for all, not only for himself, but for all the folk living around so that they could all live in a safe and secure environment without having to worry about a great wicked predator roaming around ready to pounce.

He picked up the basket and small bonnet belonging to Claudette; the flowers had all withered and were now completely dry. He stood for some time staring at the little pink bonnet with sadness and guilt. He had had no control over the forces that had pushed him against all his better judgement.

He would hide the basket and bonnet inside the small room in the loft. He walked up the wooden steps, opened the door and peered into the darkened room waiting for his eyes to become accustomed to the darkness and then he saw Claudette laid out on a small cot sleeping peacefully; he could hear the gentle rhythmic sound of her breathing.

Suddenly and without warning he was enveloped in a strong net rendering him completely unable to move. In his newfound peace of mind and feeling of optimistic outlook, he had let his guard down and had failed to sense the oncoming danger of a presence nearby intent on harming him; he uttered a loud growl and attempted to draw his sword but was swiftly dealt with a severe blow to the back of his head. He then fell heavily backwards, flashes of light passing before his eyes, struggling as the darkness crept over him like a swirling mist, threatening to choke the very life out of him.

The darkness filled all his senses and he was lost in the impenetrable blackness so thick and heavy, he was powerless to move. He groaned as he lay there squinting as he strained to see anything beyond the thick rope imprisoning him; he felt like a snared animal. He then felt another blow to his head, this time with more force and an intense sharp pain washed over him and then he lost consciousness.

When he slowly regained consciousness some time later, he found himself in a vast chilling dungeon; the walls were made of old stone with thick damp moss growing between the cracks. His head throbbed with pain and he could feel sticky thick blood oozing down his back. He peered around the dungeon hardly able to see clearly in the semi darkness except for a glow of light above.

When he looked up he could see great wrought iron candelabras swinging from side to side ominously as if threatening to crash down on him, a dribble of candle wax sometimes dripping down on his face.

He was no longer restrained in the tangled net, but his hands were now bound behind his back and there was a chain around his neck; he fought back instinctive fear but remained still as he felt a presence advancing towards him from the shadows behind the gigantic stone pillars in the dungeon. The rope burned into his wrists as he twisted and struggled frantically to loosen them. He attempted to move forward but the chain around his neck shackled to one wall held him back nearly choking him.

He heard a deep raucous laugh and then he saw a tall but slightly twisted but dominant figure appear out of the darkness advancing towards him. He felt powerless to move; his eyes strained to focus on the figure. He struggled vigorously again to free himself of the rope but it seemed to tighten its hold on him even more.

Blazing red eyes filled with hate glared at him; a violent shiver ran down his spine as a dense suffocating feeling of dread washed over him. He slowly and deliberately leaned forward, aware of the horror that skulked in the impenetrable darkness in the corner of the room.

The massive creature's eyes glowed with pure menace, the great snout flared, snorting and blowing its rage just a few feet from his face. The shadowy figure was covered with a loose cloak and although the face was partially obscured, he knew that face; there was no mistaking that evil face. Every muscle in his body tensed and he felt himself quiver not only in fear but a pure undulated feeling of rage bubbled up inside of his heart.

'You have never been able to defeat me; I outsmart you every time, don't I. I bet you are kicking yourself now that you let your defences down for those split seconds. You poor vain fool, don't you know that I am one step ahead of you every time; I know what you are thinking and what you are going to do before you even make a move.'

Dargo roared with rage as he pulled himself on his knees and lurched at the shadowy figure but stumbled and fell flat on his face, the chain rattling around his neck; he could taste the gritty dust and damp moss in his mouth.

He felt a great boot on his back pressing him even closer to the ground; his chest was heaving as he struggled to breathe spluttering out particles of dust and moss stuck to his lips.

'I need to keep you out of my way; I don't want these constant interruptions from you. I am tired of swatting you out of my way like a small irritating insect buzzing around my face. You are pathetic and now I am going to see that you will just quietly disappear. Nobody will know of your existence in this great fortress of mine and as I have also relieved you of your magnificent weighty wings you will slowly lose all your strength. But don't worry I will see that small crusts of bread are thrown to you from time to time and some water is provided for you. Your suffering will be long and agonizing but the end will slowly and finally come to you. You have served your purpose and I no longer need you.'

Dargo lay prostrate on the floor still spitting out small gritty bits of dirt and dust from his lips. He was aware of the excruciating pain on his back – the thought of losing his wings was like a death sentence to him. His head slumped forward; feeling totally helpless and hopeless of ever being able to escape from this place.

'This way, you understand, I can be very sure that you will no more interfere in my business,' the dark creature above him repeated again in a hoarse gravelly voice.

'If you could just get your great boot off of my back, I could then try to stand up and face you.'

'By all means,' the creature told him as he pulled him back up by the chain secured around of his neck nearly choking him. Dargo squinted in the darkness trying to get a clear look at the face but cried out again as he felt a sharp stabbing in his chest as the dark figure slammed his fist into him.

'What did you do with the girl?' he asked in a rasping voice hardly able to breathe now.

'Don't you mean, what did you do with the girl,' he replied. 'Don't forget it was you who led her away back to your cottage. But anyway I had better be on my way now – I am very busy and have a lot to do. I've had quite enough fun on your behalf for the day,' the dark figure whispered in Dargo's ear pushing him to the ground again, roaring with laughter.

Dargo rolled over groaning – he felt like his body had been violated and ravaged by an all-consuming poisonous substance saturating and suffocating his every sense to the point of losing all control. He was in excruciating pain hardly able to move. He lay there in a complete catatonic state of half consciousness and as his mind began to wander he felt his body spinning into another place.

He swooped down to the part of the forest where he last saw his beautiful wife and daughter. He looked around sadly at the desolate ground – It had been robbed of its natural beauty and life; the dry earth seemed to cry out for nourishment. Gone were the days when the woodlands had been a stunning, lush scene of gigantic trees swaying in the breeze, resplendent wild flowers, bursting buds and foliage.

'Not so now,' Dargo mumbled to himself. 'The Troll Warrior has seen to that – THAT DEVIL,' he cried out angrily in the wilderness of his garbled unconscious state. He didn't care who heard him, but then he knew that there was nobody around to hear him.

His voice echoed back to him in the very darkness of his soul, sounding distorted, like the roar of an enraged dragon.

He watched from the ground as his soul floated above his twisted and crushed earthly body like a great silver spirit of the skies.

He looked down at the stream below and saw a reflection of Petra with their daughter sleeping in her arms in the stillness of the water – poor Pearl; she looked so frail and pitiful.

'I must go to them now and give them renewed strength,' he whispered to himself.

He closed his eyes and called out to her, 'Petra, my own beloved wife – come to me and I will breathe strength into your soul and body and together we will be strong.'

He spread his great wings and swooped high into the air, his magnificent body glistening as he soared through the sky.

He descended into a dark area of a grey garden where she was waiting for him as if in a trance; her arms extended out to him like a small child crying out for her mother. He went to her immediately and gathered her small delicate body into his arms and embraced her against his chest. The pure warmth and strength flowed from his body into her small frame and her translucent face began to glow; her eyes glistened with huge tears that rolled down her face.

Petra looked up into Dargo's handsome face and whispered, 'You must let go now Dargo and be strong for yourself – we are both in a safe place now and we want you to be strong for yourself.'

Her tiny wisp of a face had been drained of its rosy glow and bloom of youth; she had been a sprig of a young peasant girl and had been robbed of her life and vitality. He remembered when she had first seen her dancing around the woodlands with a carefree heart and flowers in her hair.

Dargo lifted her, almost crushing her against him. 'I cannot Petra – I cannot.' He hung his head as the tears rolled down his face and dripped from his chin.

'Please don't cry, my beloved husband,' she replied.

She seemed to be enshrouded in a veil of invisible manacles attached to her heart, body and soul.

Dargo stroked her long dark hair away from her face and pressed his lips against her moist cheek. Petra buried her face in his neck and as he closed his eyes he felt a burst of strength pouring into his mind and body. He felt his mind and body gently spinning and then his eyes suddenly snapped open and he was fully awake and alone again.

At that moment he heard high-pitched demonic laughter surrounding him, nearly deafening him. The Troll Warrior could always smell his feelings of utter torment and wretchedness.

'I'm coming for you, you wretched despicable old relic,' he yelled at the top of his voice. 'Yes, that's right, because that's what you are, an evil old relic. When this is all over, you will see that you have become just a shrunken withered old evil bat.'

'You will die for that,' the demonic voice screamed back at him. When this is all over, it is you who will become just a broken withered old man.'

Dargo shook himself violently as if trying to cast off poisonous spider cobwebs that seemed to cling to his body and mind, threatening to choke the very life out of him. He tried desperately to move but he had lost all feeling. The dry cracked ground around where Dargo lay seemed to vibrate with the Troll Warrior's rage.

Chapter Twenty-Three

It was disgustingly early in the morning when Gilroy woke up feeling extremely groggy with an explosive pounding headache; his tongue felt like a huge swollen lumpy slug stuck to the roof of his mouth and his bloodshot eyes were like two fireballs in his head threatening to erupt from their very sockets.

He was puzzled why he had woken up so early, especially as they hadn't gone to sleep until really late last evening, or was it really early this same morning. He noticed immediately that Bogey was no longer beside him and he staggered up from the sofa a little too quickly, reeling over onto the floor groaning in pain. He eased himself back onto the sofa where he lay trying to muster up his strength to move again. He needed some strong hot coffee to bring him back to his senses.

He had been robbed of a restful sleep by a reoccurring nightmare involving one of his greatest youthful fears of running naked through the woods in all his splendor exposing warts and all. He shuddered at this thought as he peered around the room, trying to gather up all his strength to raise himself up from the sofa again, willing his aching body into motion.

He rolled over and stood up unsteadily, stumbling clumsily into one of the bedrooms where he could see Bogey with two of the Pug brothers scattered around lying on the carpeted floor; they were fast asleep and snoring loudly.

One of the Pug brothers, Cecil was grinning stupidly in his sleep muttering and clasping his hands together gleefully. Cedric was lying flat on his back with his legs in the air frantically moving in a cycling movement.

Gilroy stood for a moment watching this absurd farcical scene before stepping back and suddenly flying into the air, falling onto his backside with a thump. He sat dazed for a few minutes before fumbling around on the floor trying to stand up again, when his hand brushed against a small round object which went spinning across the carpeted floor. He stood up and slowly moved cautiously towards the object; he nearly gagged when he discovered that it was Cecil's glass eye, which had obviously shot out during the course of their drunken evening antics. He knelt down repressing a shudder as he picked up the small glass ball that seemed to stare at him accusingly, and placed it by the side of Cecil.

He crept out of the bedroom and walked back into the living room where Claude was still slung over the sofa, fast asleep with his spindly crooked legs askew hanging over one end of the sofa. He then padded into the kitchen for a glass of water and an aspirin for his throbbing head. He placed the tablet in his mouth behind his thickened tongue nearly choking in the process and then took a huge gulp of water, swallowing it all down with a grimace. He stood there swaying for a few minutes trying to clear his throat, fighting back a pang of nausea, shuffling awkwardly from one foot to the other.

After braving a very quick cold shower, he then prepared himself a double Espresso. He sighed as he looked at Clancy laid out on top of the kitchen table, his arms and legs dangling over the side, still wearing his beloved sequined high heels. He had obviously helped himself to too much of their ginger beer and he would certainly suffer for that later when he awoke. But in the meantime, Gilroy pushed him off of the table with one swipe of his hand.

Clancy moaned in annoyance, glared up at Gilroy and quickly rolled over underneath the table to continue his sleep, mumbling profanities.

'That was most unkind of you darling,' he muttered in between his unsavoury swear words.

As Gilroy stumbled back out of the kitchen he noticed that Claude was now laying on the floor behind the kitchen door, bundled up in blankets so that only his head was visible with his mouth wide open, saliva trickling down his chin.

'Talk about sleeping beauty,' he whispered under his breath chuckling to himself before wandering back to his own bedroom to enjoy another cup of Espresso in peace and serenity. When he had finished his coffee he stretched himself out under the bedspread and buried his head into the pillow, waiting for the awful headache to disappear.

'Oih sweet pea,' he heard a whisper in his ear a little later. He slowly began to awaken, his head still buried in the pillow; he must have dozed off and gone into a deep sleep. He then felt someone blowing into his ear.

'Wake up handsome sweet smelling boy,' he then heard a voice saying but a little louder now.

'What, who is that?' he groaned, his voice muffled by the pillow as his face was buried deep in the fabric of the pillow.

'One, two...' he heard someone again whisper and then suddenly Bogey, together with the Pug brothers shouted at the tops of their voices.

'THREE – here goes clever!' they all screamed as they jumped onto the bed. Their bodies were on top of Gilroy's, crushing him deeper and deeper into the soft mattress. He had to laugh, although he felt like pounding them all into a pulp. He swung his legs around from the side of the bed and stood up.

'Right who is fit for cooking breakfast this bright morning?' His headache had subsided now and he felt full of beans. He strutted around the room like a peacock and began to do some resemblance of stretching exercises in his boxer pants much to the amusement of the others who stood looking at him with a mixture of concern and scorn;

the very sight of him making them feel positively dizzy.

'Would you please stop that,' snorted Bogey impatiently but grinning from ear to ear.

A deep voice rumbled from the doorway. 'What on earth is going on in here? Can't a man get a decent sleep in this God forsaken place without being rudely awakened by you bunch of slobs.'

They all turned to look at Claude who had dragged himself up from the floor by the doorway of the kitchen. They looked on with a mixture of shock and pity at his grizzly appearance which far outdid even Gilroy's early morning stunning appearance. His usually slicked back hair was dangling over his face like black spider legs and huge bags erupted from underneath his eyes. His chin had developed a murky looking shadow of stubble; he looked positively frightening.

Gilroy shook his head in mock horror and disbelief, his eyes rolling but he then smiled and his expression turned thoughtful. He narrowed his eyes at Claude and his expression changed to that of an appreciative, proud glance. He suddenly had an immense feeling of respect and friendship for this weird looking poor excuse for a man and he knew that it was a mutual feeling between the two of them. He shrugged, then walked over to Claude and began patting his shoulder affectionately and then planting a big slobbering kiss on the top of his greasy head.

'Sorry me old fruit but now that you are up and awake, how about preparing breakfast for us?' he asked with a mischievous grin spreading over his face.

Claude grimaced sleepily, snorted disdainfully and then shrugged. 'Why not but please do not call me your old fruit,' he then replied nonchalantly.

'Well OK me old vegetable' Gilroy replied laughing.

Gilroy had heard that Claude suffered bouts of black moods and usually they began with spells of excessive sulking but there was no place for such emotions living with Gilroy and Bogey. He would soon get such self-indulgent nonsense knocked out of him.

They all quickly began to get busy scurrying around; the Pug brothers began tidying up the messy sitting room while Claude started preparing a delicious breakfast for them of toast, scrambled eggs and bacon. When they had all showered and the Pug brothers had also been dragged kicking and screaming to the shower, they all sat down around the table enjoying the food and company, laughing and forgetting all the bad foreboding troubles that threatened them all, especially Gilroy.

Again, they failed to notice a sinister face that suddenly appeared at the window scrutinizing them, all but one of them. Clancy had seen the ominous shadow out of the corner of his eye and when he caught clear sight of the face of the dark shadow, he gasped and quickly looked towards Gilroy; he was taken aback feeling completely ill at ease and totally baffled by the image that he had just seen. He shuddered violently as a feeling of dread and foreboding evil about to befall on them washed over him.

Gilroy caught the strange startled multiple expressions galloping over Clancy's face, a mixture of puzzlement, terror, anger and dread. It was like watching a movie in slow motion and Gilroy sat watching him, his forehead wrinkling in confusion and disconcertment.

'What is it Clancy, you look as if you have seen a ghost.'

Clancy sat there almost in a frozen state with his mouth wide open; he was momentarily shocked, confused, overwhelmed and unable to think clearly for a few split seconds.

'I don't know about a ghost darling but it looked like a mirror image of you Gilroy,' he replied when he had recovered from the shock of seeing the image at the window, his face had turned quite pale.

'I tell you sweet socks, it scared the heeby jeebies out of me.'

Both Gilroy and Claude immediately turned and looked at each other, their eyes narrowing suspiciously, then both stood up from the table and rushed to the window almost knocking each other over but the shadow had disappeared just as quickly as it had appeared.

'What exactly did you see?' Gilroy asked turning to Clancy from the window.

'I told you darling, it was a mirror image of you peering through the window looking at us; it was just the most horrible face,' Clancy replied earnestly.

Bogey and the other two Pug brothers began to chuckle but were quickly silenced by Gilroy's somber worried expression as he glared at them.

The air in the room thickened, outside the wind rose and leaves and broken branches whirled fiendishly. Branches pelted the outside walls of their cottage within the secret boundary as the wind rattled ominously at the windows. The room was unexpectedly and strangely silent as they all looked at each other collectively holding their breath.

Chapter Twenty-Four

The magnificent black horse galloped on further and further into the deepest and darkest part of the forest. Dargo sat behind Claudette with one hand around her waist holding onto her tightly and the other holding onto the reins guiding the horse on. She held her head down as the wind and rain lashed against her face almost blinding her.

'Do not be afraid my dear, we are nearly there,' he whispered in her ear.

Claudette remained silent; she felt a mixture of fear and puzzlement now. She wondered why she was being transported to such a faraway place where she knew nobody would be able to find her. Although she had been afraid being kept locked up in Dargo's cottage, she had felt a false sense of security being so close to the cottage she shared with Gruntle. She kept telling herself that she would not come to any harm with Dargo; after all he was known to be a hero in the village.

But, this man was not the same man – he was not the mysterious creature with the magnificent silver wings that she had heard so much about. She gasped now when she realized something that she had not even noticed before. He no longer had those beautiful silver white wings. She suddenly stiffened at this thought now; he felt the change in her stance immediately.

'What is it my dear, are you cold. Forgive me – we should have travelled in a carriage. As soon as we arrive at the fortress, I will see to it that a roaring fire is made up in your room. I promise you, you will be very comfortable. My manservant is arranging a sumptuous meal on your arrival. I have a surprise for you and I think you will be very pleased.'

The huge rambling fortress suddenly loomed up before them dark and ominous concealed behind huge gnarled trees that seemed to sway almost malevolently in the strong wind that had built up along the way during their journey.

When he dismounted and pushed open the heavy iron gates, she swallowed nervously as he pulled her down from the horse and mounted the steps carrying her in his arms through the huge wooden door with metal studs.

A sinister looking servant man greeted them on the other side.

'Take my cloak Baldric,' Dargo demanded. 'Where is Madam?' he then asked.

'She is in the kitchen waiting for you Sir,' Baldric answered with eyes downcast; his head bent forward facing his master in obedience.

When they both entered the kitchen, Claudette ran to Drasilla and hugged her tightly. She perhaps misinterpreted Drasilla's presence to mean that she had come to rescue her. Part of her was not sure that she wanted to be rescued from this handsome man who had abducted her; it had all seemed so exciting to her at first – she had found it somehow thrilling and romantic but now she wanted to go home and be with her godfather, Gruntle.

Dargo stood back watching with a cynical expression on his face; a smirk playing around the edges of his cruel lips.

'Well my dears, what a lovely little family we make and I can see that you are delighted to see each other; I will leave you both now to chat together and then we will have dinner at eight. Please dress appropriately in your best evening dresses – we like to dine here in style, as you know Drasilla. I made a concerted effort to collect and deliver all your richest gowns and jewellery to you here and you will find your entire refinery in your chamber room. If you need anything at all please feel free to summon Baldric who will serve you whatever you desire.'

Claudette now looked at Drasilla with a puzzled but anxious look on her face. Drasilla smiled nervously but winked at her trying to assure her that they were not going to be harmed.

Charming as he seemed, both Drasilla and Claudette now realized that Dargo was dangerous almost beyond imagination. That powerful body on its own was stronger than twenty ordinary men put together and although Drasilla had long admired his strength of character, she now felt nothing but pity for him.

She sat there now gazing into those lazy dark eyes, showing no sign of her horror at his sudden apparent but strange unexplainable transformation of character. She couldn't help thinking that the most disturbing of all was that his whole persona had changed from that of an honest gentle man, full of kindness to a dangerous predator.

He has lived so long hunting his enemy that he seems to enjoy danger so inexplicably and is unable to separate himself from the beast in himself that he has allowed to take over; he seems to glory in it, having no morals or conscience, she thought as she lowered her eyes quickly as if afraid that he would read her thoughts

They were trapped here with him in the middle of nowhere high in the hills; Drasilla knew not where he had imprisoned them. The man servant had prepared a great comforting roaring fire in the large kitchen, the coal crackled merrily in the fireplace but all to no avail as there was no comfort or merriment in the room or her heart.

Claudette and Drasilla sat at the kitchen table holding hands; Drasilla was surprised to see that Claudette was extremely calm although tired after the journey that day. She deliberately suppressed her surprise when she saw that Claudette's hair had turned completely white so as not to alarm her.

'Are you alright my dear?' Drasilla asked her gently pushing back tendrils hanging across her face.

'Yes, I am fine Drasilla.'

'Have you not noticed,' Claudette then whispered to her.

'Not noticed what?' Drasilla replied looking puzzled. She sat looking at her for a few seconds. 'Oh yes, your hair – it has gone completely white; I thought you were a ghost at first. How did that happen?' Drasilla then asked her.

'No, no, that's not what I am referring. No, I mean he has no wings. I've only just realized – how could I have not noticed that before,' she whispered again.

'We'll talk later,' Drasilla whispered back when she heard Dargo coming back down the hallway.

He came through the doorway carrying two glasses of sherry, vivid amber in color that glowed brightly in the darkness of the room; she instantly smelt the aromas of fine wood and hazelnuts with a hint of orange peel. She watched him quietly and intently as he walked towards her smiling; his handsome face full of malice. He handed first one glass to her and the other to Claudette who declined to accept it.

Claudette sat there in silence while they ate dinner in the great opulent dining room. Both Drasilla and Claudette had changed into elegant evening gowns as requested by their host. Claudette had been hopeful of the situation when she had first seen Drasilla but now on seeing her worried expression and body language, she realized that there was certainly something sinister going on.

Chapter Twenty-Five

His afternoon nap was rudely interrupted when he opened his eyes and found himself staring at a dripping slobbering canine snout. Claude attempted to raise himself up from the sofa, trying to push the dog off, but the massive paws planted firmly on his chest rendered him solidly pinned prostrate on the sofa. He frantically shook his head from side to side in an effort to stop the slobbery onslaught of face licking.

'Come here boy,' Errol shouted from the doorway.

Wally immediately bounded over to Errol in obedience to the command.

'How did you get in here?' Claude asked in a hoarse whisper as he gingerly laid his head back down on the sofa and resumed lying motionless as he stared up at Errol whose face etched with hostility now positioned itself in Claude's line of vision, his arms crossed rigidly in front of his chest and legs astride in an authoritative but intimidating stance.

'If you could just give me a little space here, I'll stand up and we can discuss this like two civilized people,' Claude said as he struggled to prop himself up on his elbows.

Errol's arrogant condescending manner made Claude feel nervous as he continued to loom over him, refusing to move out of the way, his fixed gaze was like a deadly weapon slicing through to his very mind.

'Excuse me,' Claude grumbled as he eased himself sideways from the sofa and hauled himself to his feet, gingerly but nervously sidling around Errol, apologetically shoving him aside in the process. He couldn't abide such a display of obvious indulgent self-importance; in addition to being extremely handsome and popular, Errol was extremely vain. He seemed to lack even the tiniest bit of empathy for the less than pure or anyone who did not measure up to the degree of his own personal outstanding qualities, according to his view that is.

It annoyed Claude a great deal that Errol seemed to live an infinite auspicious lifestyle marked by luck and good omens promising never ending success and happiness.

Besides all that, he always ended up with the most attractive maiden and it didn't seem at all fair to others who were far less fortunate. In fact, just the thought of Errol's seemingly privileged existence made the muscles of Claude's stomach launch into a series of involuntary spasms causing him to want to throw up. It was not that he begrudged him anything and he was the type of person who was delighted at another person's good fortune and happiness; it was just that Errol was so conceited and full of self-importance to the point of being exasperatingly and nauseatingly irritating.

Claude's face was a picture of pure disconcertment; his feelings of discomfort and inadequacy threatening to engulf him as he stood there in front of this near perfect haughty man.

Errol was unperturbed by Claude's obvious disgruntlement and his less than happy demeanor at seeing him.

'Where is he then?' he asked, finally speaking and looking Claude straight in the eyes menacingly and making that clicking sound with his tongue.

'Where is who?' Claude replied visibly flinching. He had always detested any confrontation in any form and always tried to avoid having to deal with fights whether physical or verbal.

'Don't act the simpleton with me Claude, I am quite aware that you do lack some degree of intelligence and common sense but I know you are not completely dense. You are already in a lot of trouble, not to mention being disloyal to Drasilla, which is despicable to begin with. It is absolutely clear to me now that you are an accessory in her abduction and I am going to have to take you into custody.'

'Whatever I am or whatever you think I am, I have never been disloyal to Madam, nor will I ever be – Madam will vouch for that, I can assure you,' he replied indignantly. He was infuriated that Errol would accuse him of such a thing; he was guilty of many things but never betrayal to Madam; why he had never even contemplated one single act of disloyalty or dishonesty towards her; he would rather cut his right arm off.

'Well, I hardly think she can vouch for you at the moment since we have been unable to locate her whereabouts, unless you can help us with our investigation at this point, in which case, you can help yourself. Why don't you start by telling us where we can find Gilroy; it's not doing you any good trying to protect him and the longer he goes on the run, the more difficult it will be for him to hide. There will always be someone who will hunt him down for a substantial reward and I have to say that we have enlisted the assistance of the leader of the Globs, who as you know is a sworn enemy of Gilroy's.'

'Listen, you've got this all wrong as usual, we are all trying to tell you that Gilroy is not the one you should be searching for. You have to understand that the whole situation is very complicated beyond imagination,' Claude said clenching his spindly hands into fists.

Errol cocked his head to one side, eyes narrowing. He sighed and turned away from Claude and walked over to the window peering out on hearing a commotion outside. Wally also heard the commotion and bounded to the window barking furiously and loudly.

'I am tired of listening to the same old story – I have not got this all wrong as you say and there is nothing complicated about this; it is quite simple...,' Errol stopped suddenly in mid-sentence as he now turned towards the door.

Claude glared at him still clenching his fists.

The door was flung open again and in walked Gruntle followed by several of Errol's officers of law, two of whom held onto Gilroy before shoving him forward roughly. Gilroy stumbled into the room, his hands cuffed behind his back. He looked deflated, sighing heavily looking up from one face to another, sprawled on the ground, gasping for breath. A howl of frustration and agony erupted from his throat and his heart hammered threatening to jump out of his throat; his head slumped forward as he feigned unconsciousness.

'So at last we have you and you can stop your little game Gilroy, I know you are conscious,' Errol said with a glint in his eye. 'And, I must say it didn't prove too difficult at all to track you down this time with the help of Wally,' he continued as he petted Wally's head.

Wally suddenly broke away from the side of Errol and bounded towards Gilroy knocking one of the officers of law over in his haste to get to him. He straddled him on the floor licking his face all over, his tail all the while wagging with happiness at seeing his old friend.

'Well somebody is pleased to see him and I must say Wally I am disappointed with you, I would have thought that you could have immediately smelt him out seeing as he was practically under your nose. Where did you find him?' Errol then asked as he walked over to the two men standing over Gilroy who then yanked him up back on his feet from the floor.

'In the outside lavatory and it wasn't difficult to sniff him out. It couldn't have been easier; it was like sniffing out a skunk with his pants down,' quipped one of the officers of law with an obvious smirk on his face.

'Oh very funny and I must say that I don't appreciate being disturb like that – It's not very polite at all, I must say, especially as they hardly gave me a chance to pull my pants up – it's totally uncivilized,' Gilroy said huffing and puffing and grunting indignantly. 'You have a most disagreeable and uncultured group of men working with you Errol.'

'Oh and you are certainly not vulgar Gilroy in any way or form are you? But anyway I am not going to stand here talking to garbage such as yourself. Get him out of here and take him back to the station,' he then said turning to the two officers of law who then dragged him back out through the door.

'And, you come with...,' he started to say as he turned back to where Claude had been standing but during all the commotion, he had quietly slipped out while all attention had been focused on Gilroy.

'Get on after him,' he yelled at some of the other officers of law. 'He may lead us straight to where Drasilla and Claudette are being held.'

As he followed Gilroy being led out of the door, Errol suddenly turned and realized that Gruntle had not said a single word the whole time, realizing now that he had also just as silently slipped out during all the commotion when Gilroy had been apprehended.

'Come here boy,' he called out and then whistled for Wally but he had also gone.

He stood there scratching his head and sighing in exasperation, he was surrounded by idiots. There was certainly something very, very funny going on here but he was going to find out exactly what it was. He realized that anger and frustration had been building up in Gruntle over the last few days and he could understand that he was intent on finding Claudette as quickly as possible, but he was going the wrong way about it.

He had also been baffled over the last few days by the disappearance of Dargo; it wasn't like Dargo to suddenly and inexplicably completely vanish without contacting him.

'Where has that damn man got to,' he mumbled to himself clicking his tongue inside his mouth repeatedly. 'This certainly does not look good for him – it's all very suspicious and damning evidence.'

Unless he had decided to go on a mission by himself, but, then again, he would have at least given some idea of where he was going, he thought to himself.

As proud as Dargo was, Errol knew that he always talked over things with him and Errol just knew that Dargo would have somehow alerted him to where he was going if he possibly could. Errol did not like to think the worst but with Dargo just disappearing like that suddenly worried him.

As he stood there on his own contemplating all the events that had taken place over the last few days to his knowledge, he suddenly had a feeling that he was maybe being kept out of the loop here; somebody was concealing something from him. His eyes narrowed in suspicion.

There is definitely something fishy afoot here, he thought to himself, his brow wrinkling and his eyes narrowing.

'But I will certainly find out exactly what is going on here,' he muttered to himself as he now strode out of the door. The whole area was now quiet after all the commotion apart from the birds singing in the trees. He looked around suspiciously almost expecting something or somebody to jump out from behind one of the trees. He walked over to the outside privy but decided not to go inside as the smell pervading around it almost made him gag and threatened to render him unconscious.

'The way some people live,' he muttered to himself as he began marching quickly along the secret pathway away from Gilroy's cottage.

'Now where did they all go,' he said between gritted teeth, he was slowly beginning to feel at boiling point.

'I am the Sheriff here and I am in charge.' He growled, crossing his arms, clearly annoyed, more than he could say.

Chapter Twenty-Six

The sun shone brightly that morning accompanied by a low swirling mist that blanketed everywhere with a morning dew sparkling like tiny diamonds on the leaves of the trees and the grass.

The Pug brothers ran as fast as their little stumpy legs could carry them sometimes slipping and sliding on the soggy moss carpeted ground whooping and hollering in complete hysteria.

They had watched the hullabaloo through all the great gnarled trees surrounding Gilroy's hideaway. They had been on their way to give Gilroy some important information but were too late to even get to Claude in time before his rude awakening.

When they had now reached a spot where they felt safe from Errol and his officers of law, they threw themselves to the ground collapsing in a heap gasping and panting in their sheer panic and exhaustion.

The brothers' senses were on high alert for all sounds in the woodland as they now sat bolt upright still panting. They could hear a dog barking in the distance and then the sound of someone running, shouting instructions. They threw themselves flat to the ground again, their bodies quivering with fear; they tried to remain motionless although Cedric could not help his teeth from clattering so loud that it sounded like horses galloping.

Clancy's scrawny stumpy little hands fidgeted with irritation, his own teeth grinding together as he glared at Cedric. His desire to wring Cedric's neck was overpowering;

'Would you stop that, you idiot,' Clancy whispered hoarsely. 'Do you want them to find us as well and drag us off to their station? Is that what you want aay, aay?' he demanded, his voice almost rising to an hysterical scream.

'Nnnnnno and please don't shout at me,' Cedric stuttered, now shaking even more violently. To make matters worse he had developed hic-cups; he always had the hic-cups when he became extremely anxious. He felt as if his head was going to fall off of his body and he placed his hands firmly over his ears to ensure that it wouldn't.

Trying hard to calm himself, Cedric closed his eyes tightly and sank deep into the thick damp moss as if trying to disappear completely from sight.

They drew in their breath sharply, when through the bushes they now saw several pairs of feet appear standing nearby where they were hiding.

'Now see what you've done, you idiot,' Clancy hissed through his teeth, glaring at Cedric, his hands held out claw-like in front of him; he felt an uncontrollable urge to throttle him again.

'I know they are somewhere around here,' they heard a voice now say. 'They left earlier this day to track down the figure they saw at the window yesterday.'

'Clancy – are you here,' the voice now whispered. 'It's OK, you can come out now. Gruntle, Claude and Wally are here with me and we can do this together.'

The Pug brothers reared up their heads simultaneously surprised at hearing Gilroy's voice. They had seen it with their own eyes; they had seen him being dragged out of the cottage with his hands handcuffed behind his back.

They leapt over the bushes in their haste to get to Gilroy; Clancy shoved Cedric sideways, causing him to topple over backwards arms akimbo. He lay flat on his back staring up at Gilroy wide eyed.

'Is that really you?' Clancy asked prodding and poking him and then springing up and throwing his arms around Gilroy's portly stomach.

'Yes, it really is me,' Gilroy answered clapping him on his back affectionately grinning from ear to ear.

'But how did you escape? We saw you being bundled off between the two Officers of Law.'

'Well if you must know, between Gruntle here and Claude, they managed to overcome Errol's Officers of Law and free me. Gruntle here understands now that there is a more evil force behind this to deal with.'

'Well alright then,' Claude now said emphatically. 'Let's get this show on the road and reveal all.'

'First of all,' said Gruntle, 'tell us what you have discovered and take us to the secret hideaway.'

'It's quite some distance but if we keep going we could reach the location early tomorrow morning but we must be sure to stick together and not lose sight of each other because we are about to go through dark and damp parts of the forest.'

As they marched on keeping close together as much as they could, they all became aware that the closer the got to the great hidden fortress how dangerous the route was and every step they took threatened them with deadly snakes and poisonous thorns jutting out at every turn.

When they finally arrived at the foreboding fortress, Gruntle followed stealthily behind as Gilroy moved swiftly through the never-ending passageways; for one so clumsy and heavy, he was surprised that Gilroy was so light on his feet. He turned to see Claude and the Pug brothers close behind in a single line; their faces set in deadly serious expressions of fear and dread of the unknown.

He tried to stifle his feeling of irritation at seeing the Pug brothers; they were such numb heads and were sure to give them away in their important mission at hand. They constantly tripped over their own feet and each-other and seemingly could not help themselves from yelping and grunting as they stumbled along behind. *But after all,* he thought to himself, *they did find the location of this secret fortress which he hoped would lead them straight to Claudette and for that he was thankful to them at least.*

He smiled as he then saw Wally, faithful Wally, his tread as silent as a lamb as he padded close behind them all panting, his tongue hanging out. It was Wally who had caused him to change his mind about Gilroy; when he had seen how the dog had shown so much affection for him, he realized that Gilroy could not possibly be the dark and sinister monster he had thought him to be.

They continued moving cautiously along the never ending long dark passageways of the fortress and if it wasn't for glimpses of the moon, which occasionally shone through the heavy brocade curtaining at the windows, they would have hardly been able to see one foot in front of the other.

Hardly a word passed between them as they trudged on with quick blundering steps sometimes stumbling over worn threadbare carpeting but all the while keeping a vigilant look-out.

Skulking alongside the blank and dreary damp walls, Gilroy who was now a little in advance of them, stopped before a door, and pushing it open, entered through to another wing of the fortress.

They could hear the sound of music floating throughout from the upper part of the castle. Gruntle now remained right behind Gilroy until they reached an arched entryway leading to a stone stairway where they found Bogey waiting grudgingly, crouched shivering and looking decidedly cantankerous and frustrated.

'About time too,' he rasped, 'I've been waiting that long in this dusty old place and I'm so parched I could drink a few cans of ginger beer. This place is creepy, I can tell you that and I am frozen through to my bones,' he continued shivering and rubbing his hands together.

'Oh stop ya moaning will ya, just be thankful that I made it at all. You could have been waiting a lot longer; that pesky Sheriff came over uninvited and literally ambushed me sitting on me throne in me privy – it comes to something when a man can't even sit peacefully and have a quiet dump on his own lavatory. But I outsmarted him as usual,' Gilroy replied looking extremely pleased with himself.

'I'm surprised that the stink didn't knock them all out; it usually works like that with me,' Bogey said with a sneer on his face.

'Ok, that's enough you two – never mind about all that – this is no time for flippancy. This is serious business and there is no time for joking, let's move; we can't be hanging around all day twittering and tweeting amongst ourselves, we've got an important mission here,' growled Gruntle.

They all climbed down the dark stone stairway leading straight to a heavy iron grated door, which in turn lead them into a huge cellar area with a large hearth where a roaring fire blazed fiercely almost lighting up the whole room. The musty dank smell which pervaded from within immediately filled their nostrils and flooded their senses with dread.

The marble stonework walls within the cellar were black from smoke and dirt and grime covered the stone flooring. Although the cellar was mostly in darkness, there were huge candelabras swinging from the ceiling and droplets of burning wax dripped down.

'Where are we?' Clancy muttered clamping his hand over his mouth because of the smell.

'This is a dungeon where prisoners and an army of rats are probably kept,' Gilroy replied mockingly, his mind seeming to be a little distracted as his nostrils flared. He had a distinct feeling that they were not alone.

'Oooh darling, please don't mention rats – they give me the willies and heeby jeebies.'

'Will you just stop your prattling you half-wit. Why did you bring them with us in the first place Gilroy; they are just a nuisance and of no use to us whatsoever,' Gruntle said gruffly, forgetting how helpful they had been so far.

'Don't be unkind Gruntle – they have been extremely useful to us and you know...,' Gilroy started to say but was interrupted by a scratching sound.

'Can you see the rats darling, can you, can you?' Clancy screeched as he hurled himself into the arms of Gruntle who immediately tossed him onto the floor with disgust.

'I'm warning you, if you don't stop your nonsense, I'm going to turn you into a rat and then you can scuttle off with the rest of them and live happily ever after.'

'Oooh you are wicked darling, but I like you,' Clancy replied as he dragged himself off the floor and brushed himself down. 'Oooh, the dust in here; it's positively disgusting.'

'Shush you two, I'm trying to listen here,' Gilroy hissed.

From a darkened corner on the far side of the cellar, they suddenly heard grunting noises and the sound of iron chains rattling.

'Aaaagh, it's a ghost darling – quick pumpkins let's get out of here,' Clancy suddenly screamed out, his little pudgy body shaking violently as he turned to bolt, dragging Cedric and Cecil with him.

The Pug brothers immediately ran back up the stairs and huddled together like three frightened fawns at the top of the stairway and then seemed to disappear out of sight.

Gruntle rolled his eyes shrugging his shoulders unsympathetically, reiterating his judgment of the Pug brothers.

Wally bounded over to the spot where the grunting was coming from followed by Gilroy, where they found what looked to be a bundle of tattered dirty garments.

When Gilroy looked closer he could see a twisted and bruised body enfolded beneath the heap of tattered and crumpled covering.

'Dargo!' he cried out, his heart wrenched when he recognized the face. Once his stomach stopped lurching, he looked around at Gruntle while gripping his hands into fists, gulping profusely, his eyes flashing in his fury at seeing Dargo in such a shocking condition; his mighty wings had been ripped from his back.

How could this happen to such a strong indestructible and indomitable force, he thought to himself. *He would not have believed it if he had not seen it for himself. But then without his powerful wings he would lose all his strength.*

Dargo could barely move from where he lay as a chain was fixed tightly around his throat rendering him almost unable to even speak; his breathing was shallow and labored and his limbs were shaking. His haggard features were that of a man starved of food and water for days on end. He had a full beard of several days' growth and wild unkempt hair matted with dirt and grime.

He struggled to open one bruised and swollen eyelid and squinted up at Gilroy who gently raised his head on his knee, produced a flask, and poured some brandy from it down his throat. After drinking some of the liquid and choking a little, Dargo looked at the group around him and groaned deeply as if in great pain.

'My God, it's really Dargo,' Gilroy whispered hoarsely turning to Gruntle. Wally began barking loudly in between licking Dargo's face frantically trying to wash all the blood encrusted grime from his skin.

'Is he dead?' Gruntle asked as he stood over Gilroy's shoulders. He bent over more closely looking down at Dargo holding a lamp towards him to peer directly into his face and perceived that his features were darkened and distorted. He was immediately shocked at his appearance. His swollen face appeared to be streaked in dirt but Gruntle feared that the dark marks were mostly bruises.

'How can he be dead you nincompoop; he's just drunk some Brandy,' Gilroy whispered angrily hardly able to contain his bad temper; he was fast losing his patience with Gruntle's apparent rapid onset of dementia which would normally amuse him in ordinary circumstances.

God help me I'm surrounded by idiots, he thought to himself.

'Who did this to you Dargo?' Gruntle now whispered. I'm so sorry to have suspected you of taking Claudette – please forgive me dear boy.'

Dargo's eyes suddenly widened as he struggled to move; he appeared to be trying to alert them all of something behind them. They all turned simultaneously and stood looking up at the stairway squinting in the darkness.

Chapter Twenty-Seven

Baldric went about his business as usual seeing that everything was running satisfactorily. The old gaunt cook and housekeeper was busy preparing a mid-day meal for the guests and the numerous cleaners had all been given instructions to carry out their usual tasks of organizing and tending to the Master's private quarters. Baldric had to regularly check on all the cleaners as they were a bunch of unreliable and undesirable individuals who were constantly having to be replaced on a monthly basis; it was very difficult to find trustworthy people for such a sinister and fear-provoking Master.

'See that the prisoner in the dungeon is given bread and water today – I don't think he will last another day without some kind of sustenance.'

'Yes but the Master has given strict instructions that he be only given water.'

'Yes, I do understand but he needs something to eat so just do as I say and take a bowl of that broth down to him with some bread,' Baldric spoke harshly.

The old cook grunted as he continued stirring the thick broth he was preparing. 'Huh, I thought you had already been down there this morning to check on him. Don't you remember when I prepared some porridge laced with a little Brandy that you took to him as soon as the Master went out for his usual walk?'

'Porridge, what porridge – laced with a little Brandy – I don't think so,' Baldric exclaimed irritated.

'And I hope you have been able to find those lost keys; I need the extra set in case the Master needs them', the old cook replied.

'Now what are you prattling on about,' Baldric said watching the old cook intently as he hobbled around the huge kitchen grunting and groaning.

'I really think you should think about retiring; you can hardly think straight these days and your food is becoming sloppy and uninspiring. I'm sure the Master would welcome a younger cook with fresh ideas – I am so sick of your thick broths and chicken stews.'

'There is nothing wrong with my chicken stews. You can't beat a good basic old-fashioned stew with onions, carrots, celery and garlic with just a sprinkling of wine to entice the taste buds.'

'Yes, well I need to go on about my own duties,' Baldric replied impatiently.

The old cook was after all consistently adequately reliable and had been loyal to the Master all his life. He thought to himself begrudgingly, barely unable to show willingness to bestow him the tiniest amount of praise.

And, his chicken stews and casseroles were delicious after all – he had to admit to himself. Baldric had always been a man with an ungenerous nature; his unwillingness to give somebody praise or admiration of any kind was well known to all the servants in the house but although he was strict and bad-tempered at all times, they all respected him for his fairness and basic if somewhat rarely presented gentle nature.

He strode out of the room leaving the old cook groaning and muttering to himself as he continued shuffling around the kitchen.

'I don't know what's got into him these days,' the old cook mumbled as he sat down at the table with a dish of the porridge he had made earlier.

But just as he was about to take a mouthful, he turned abruptly in the chair startled, causing his neck to wrench as Baldric suddenly returned whistling and rubbing his hands together in anticipation; his whole demeanor seeming to have altered in a matter of minutes from being bad-tempered to lighthearted.

'For goodness sake, what do you want now – you gave me such a start there blundering in here like that,' he protested. 'I nearly dropped me porridge all over me self.'

'What is that delicious smell,' Baldric said still rubbing his hands together. 'I can't wait to sample your delicious tasty broth later but for now I want you to rustle up some eggs and bacon for me this bright and fine morning; I am that famished I could eat a horse.'

'You were just saying that you were tired of my broths. I think I do need to retire – I don't know whether I am coming or going with you lot here in this morbid great mausoleum filled with soulless zombies. It's bad enough that I have to deal with a fearsome Master; I have to deal with a Jekyll and Hyde character for a footman or manservant, whatever you like to call yourself.'

He shuffled over to the cooker and grudgingly began to prepare eggs and bacon for Baldric who sat at the table still whistling, waiting patiently. When a plate of eggs and bacon where viciously slammed in front of him, he hurriedly finished his meal, stood up and strode back out of the kitchen whistling again with a contented smile upon his face and winking at the old cook before he went out of the door.

His head suddenly popped around the door again. 'What do they call you anyway other than the old cook?' Baldric now asked still grinning.

'What do they call me?' He bristled as he replied. 'I am not called anything; you know fine full well that I've always just been known as the old cook,' he continued gruffly.

'I'm just asking,' Baldric said still smiling. 'There is no harm in friendly chatter between old staff.'

'Well I don't have the time for friendly chatter with you and besides you've never shown any interest in friendly chatter before,' he mumbled looking at him suspiciously. 'Now get orf out of my kitchen and leave me alone.'

With that said Baldric withdrew his head away from the open doorway and walked off whistling again.

The old cook stood there looking puzzled before taking out a bottle of wine that he kept hidden in a cupboard for his own use only and guzzled down half the bottle before resuming his kitchen duties. When he had cleared up most of the mess in the kitchen, he flopped down on a chair sighing loudly as he started to eat the rest of his porridge.

He rolled his eyes as Baldric came stomping back into the kitchen again, his brow wrinkling in disgruntlement.

'Why are you sitting there like you have all the time in the world. Didn't I ask you to take some broth with bread and water down to the prisoner?'

'Now listen, I've had just about enough of you this morning – just get out of my kitchen and leave me alone to get on with my work. You are giving me a headache marching in and out of this kitchen non-stop like a demented jack in the box; I am beginning to get dizzy, I can tell you that. What has gotten into you for the last few days?'

'I don't know what you mean! There is nothing wrong with me old man. I am just trying to keep the place running in a respectable and orderly fashion and as you know I have to constantly keep an eye on everything and everybody here.'

'Well stop skulking around spying on me,' he replied indignantly.

'What do you mean spying on you – why would I want to spy on you?'

'I've seen you hovering outside the door watching me and the Master.'

'Don't be ridiculous, why would I have to hover outside your kitchen watching you; I've every freedom of movement in this castle and I do not need to hover or skulk around anywhere as you say.'

'Anyway, as I was saying, you need to go down to the prisoner, but before that...' He now continued but hesitated for a second before he sank down into a chair opposite the old cook.

'Come to think of it, I have not eaten this morning and am that famished I could do with a good breakfast of eggs and bacon to see me through the most part of the day.'

The old cook suddenly spluttered on his porridge as he abruptly stood up from the table so aggressively that the chair toppled over behind him. He literally stomped over to the kitchen sink, threw his dish of porridge into the sink and without a word snatched a pan and began preparing eggs and bacon for Baldric.

The man is fast losing his mind, Baldric sat there thinking. After he had hastily finished the plate of food that had been slammed in no uncertain terms begrudgingly in front of him, he stood up and marched back out of the kitchen silently without looking behind at the old cook who had stood at the far side of the kitchen all the while scowling at him. When Baldric had closed the kitchen door, the old cook hurled a wooden bowl at the door with such ferocity that it split into two making a crashing sound.

'GET OUT AND STAY OUT,' he bellowed.

Baldric visibly flinched when he heard the crashing sound behind the closed door as he continued walking along the passageway trying to ignore the ranting going on behind the closed door.

'Something has to be done about that cantankerous old crank,' he muttered to himself.

Chapter Twenty-Eight

The dark tall figure stood at the top of the stone stairway shrouded in a black cloak, staring down at them with a hatchet in his hands which glinted brightly in the darkness menacingly. The figure then began to descend the stairs slowly and when he came into closer view and his face was visible to the eye, both Gilroy and Gruntle gasped when the figure before them revealed someone who looked like Dargo but dressed in the finest attire like a prince.

When the dark figure reached the foot of the stairs, he stood off to one side, leaning on a marble column with a fiendish sardonic smirk on his face, seeming to tower over them like a gigantic demon, his eyes had a leering and malignant look.

'YOU!' Gilroy shouted, instantly recognizing the man's seemingly deceptive stance. He moved forward then stopped and stared, unable to believe that the man before him was the same evil tormenter and bully who had damaged his life and reputation as a young man almost irretrievably.

Wally immediately ran over to the figure growling and snarling, his lip curling revealing his pointed teeth. The demonic figure kicked out at Wally sending him flying across the room yelping. Wally seemed to only be winded as he slowly backed away against the darkened corner out of sight and quietly made his way back up the stone steps.

Gruntle stood back staring over at the man leaning on the marble column and then glanced back at the chained heap on the floor. His eyes narrowed as he turned to look again at the menacing figure standing before them. 'Dargo, what's going on here?' He seemed confused, suspicion darkening his brow. 'Who is that man over there?' he demanded angrily.

The man beneath the shabby covering moaned trying to speak but only a rasping sound could be heard.

Gilroy sighed loudly and rolled his eyes; he was completely losing his patience with Gruntle. *The man is just a shadow of his former self; he has a brain disorder marked by progressive and irreversible mental deterioration*, he thought as he stood up quickly hiding the flask in his jacket pocket.

'Well, my addled friend, and forgive me because I don't want to insult you, but for a so-called Magician, you don't seem to have the slightest sign of any insight into anything at all but let me explain it to you,' Gilroy now said while still looking at the dark figure standing before them. 'This man standing before us is not Dargo but an ugly Troll like me; he is in fact the diabolical Troll Warrior.'

The figure moved forward and suddenly slammed a fist into his chest pushing Gilroy with such force that he fell backwards towards the hearth, momentarily stunned.

'No, let me explain it to you; that poor delusional wreck over there has been masquerading around as me for a long, long time and I have finally imprisoned him here to put a stop to it once and for all.

He swung the hatchet in his hand menacingly from side to side as he spoke. Gruntle made to step forward but hesitated, bewilderment flickering across his face.

Gilroy remained on the dusty marble flooring after frantically trying to extinguish some flames that had attached themselves to his great behind by rolling from side to side. He bit his lip in a frenzied effort to stop himself from crying out in his pain and discomfort, at the same time aware now that the Pug brothers were crouched hovering at the top of the stairway almost out of view, but watching and listening intently.

As the dark figure standing before them wandered over to the other man enfolded in a heap on the floor, it gave Gilroy enough time to regain his senses. He stood up straight and attempted to dash forward but the figure let out a roar and lashed out knocking him backwards again.

The breath was knocked out of Gilroy as he lay sprawled out on the floor again. He scuttled back on his backside a little further as the figure advanced closer as a warning to him to stay put.

'Don't try that again or I will be forced to punish you and you won't be able to stand at all; I'll chop your legs off and you will be bouncing around on your great flatulent behind,' the dark figure said again swinging the ax menacingly from side to side.

'What are you going to do with him?' Gruntle said as he took another step forward towards the heap on the floor but stopped abruptly when he looked down to see the ax now pushed against his own chest. As he looked up into the face he was met with an evil forceful glare.

'And as for you my poor befuddled friend, if you are really good, I may let you go free but not so for that useless heap on the floor. I'm going to cut out his heart and eat it,' he said now leaning against the column again, watching them both with a fiendish grin.

'Dargo, whatever has gotten into you – you are behaving very strangely; I know things have been very difficult for you and I understand your anguish and frustration – I feel the same way myself and I want to know where Claudette is right now,' he demanded angrily. He shivered as the figure stepped even closer to him almost towering over him.

Gruntle looked around now at Gilroy who had recovered enough and was standing quietly to one side.

'Is this some sort of a nightmare, or what? Could somebody tell me exactly what is going on here?' Gruntle continued suddenly closing his eyes tightly and pressing a hand to his forehead.

'Don't let me come over there and slap some sense into you and yes, it is a nightmare and it is my living nightmare; a nightmare that I have had to endure throughout my whole life. I've told you Gruntle, GET IT INTO YOUR THICK HEAD, how many times do you need to be told that this man standing before you is NOT Dargo. This man here standing before you is my twin brother Waldobert and I have had to suffer at the hands of this evil person who bullied and tortured me when we were boys. Not only did he torment me but he tormented all the other children around and I was blamed for all his evil deeds. I have had to endure the weight of a life crippled by crime and remorse through the fault of my brother standing before us and until now I could find no means of freeing myself from it. I have dreaded this moment of being face to face with my tormenter but now I welcome it and want it to end,' he murmured almost to himself.

The dark figure suddenly flew up into the air to hover over them sneering and then laughing loudly as he floated above them like a giant black bat; his newly acquired mighty wings flapping loudly behind him.

'That's only a figment of your imagination,' he hissed. 'I am the mighty Dargo and you are just a poor bloated ugly toad who always wanted to glorify yourself in your brother's macabre reputation because you never had any courage of your own convictions yourself.'

'No, you are wrong about that; I was forced to live bounded by my brother's shame and dishonor and I had to make the best of my life and I have good friends to support me.'

'Huh, good friends you say; an ugly Hog, equally ugly Pugs and a befuddled so-called Wizard. What more could you want with a bunch of misfits like that – lucky you indeed.'

With that said he descended at the top of the stairway, spun around and stepped out of the cellar closing the thick wooden iron studded door loudly making the walls of the cellar almost shudder with the impact.

He had failed to notice the Pug brothers at the top of the stairway who had immediately scuttled off completely out of sight when he had unknowingly to himself advanced closer to them. For once they had kept utterly soundless, afraid that the slightest little sound would alert the Troll Warrior to them.

Gilroy immediately ran over to Dargo; knelt down beside him and pulled him up, but Dargo had lost consciousness and his head slumped against Gilroy's chest. Gilroy gasped when he drew the tatty cloth back to reveal that his wings had in fact been removed leaving small stumpy remnants of muscle tissue exposed.

A hand clamped on his arm. He turned to see Gruntle hovering over him staring at the mass of scars on the slumped body.

'This can't be right – this is not real,' he whispered,

'Yes it is real and now that I've finally convinced you that this man here is our Dargo, we need to get some help for him before we lose him. We can only hope that Clancy and the others find a way for us to get the hell out of this place.'

Gruntle visibly shivered. 'So how do you imagine that those three idiots are going to find a way for us to get out of here, especially in those high heels that they have taken to wearing?'

Gilroy cringed, trying not to reveal too much of his own feelings of doubt about the expectations of the Pug brothers.

'Yes well, those three idiots did actually find a way to this place – remember. Look, let's have a bit of faith here; don't forget that Claude is also wandering around somewhere up there and I suspect that Wally will be able to alert more help and is probably at this very moment making his way back to his master who will in turn surely alert Errol.'

'I think the secret is in the wings,' Gruntle now said, looking thoughtful. 'Those wings have given your twin brother power beyond his dreams – take them away and he is helpless.'

Gilroy nodded looking deep in thought. 'Yes, you are right but Waldobert's body will surely reject those wings when he reverts back to his original form and as you may have noticed Dargo has the stumps on his back still intact and his wings will grow back when his body regains strength and the blood starts pumping and surging with full force through his veins.

'But, in all this commotion did you see where Bogey went? I can't even recall if he actually followed us down into the dungeon here. I just hope nothing has happened to him.'

Chapter Twenty-nine

The dark demonic figure seemed to lose his solidity as he slowly transformed back to his former self; his demeanour had undergone a fearful change and his countenance was even paler than before; he stumbled as the power drained out of him. The longer he sustained another guise the weaker he became when he altered back to his true self. He was also beginning to lose his control over the duration of time he was able to sustain a transformation.

Within the period of several days he had transformed himself back and forth into Dargo, Claude, Gilroy and then back to himself as he had spun his tangled web of diabolical deception and he was now beginning to feel the deadly damaging impact of the changes which were slowly completely draining him and rendering him weak to the point of dangerous muscle disintegration and brain dysfunction.

He staggered and fell to his knees and a howl of pain came from his mouth as the mighty wings on his back began to contract and shrivel again – he would have to inject them again with a special serum. He crawled back through the long dark corridor until he reached the part of the castle where he knew nobody else could find him, not even his man servant. He needed time to recover in his lair located in a part of the castle via a secret tunnel, the entrance of which was almost undetectable to the eye behind a thick heavy door fitted tightly into the massive stone slabs along the cold dark passage way leading up a long winding stone flight of steps to the eaves of the castle. He clung frantically to the side railings as he struggled to reach the top, his strength nearly spent as he reached the attic.

He dragged himself over to a locked cupboard, fumbled for the key hanging around his neck, unlocked the cupboard and took one of the vials of elixir that were stored inside and drank the contents straight down. He drew in his breath as he felt the hot liquid coursing through his veins sending his muscles into violent convulsions. He was sweating profusely and began breathing more rapidly as his body started to thrash around feverishly.

The change gradually began to take place and when the muscle spasms subsided and his breathing was no longer agonizingly laborious, his own sinister demonical features began to slowly emerge.

When his breathing stabilized he stirred and pulled himself up from the floor. He walked over to his mirror; although his stance was slightly unstable he sighed with relief as he saw the old familiar reflection of himself, Waldobert the mighty Troll Warrior. He chuckled now as he brushed his bushy hair back away from his face. As twin brothers they were almost identical, both had a large bulbous nose and big pointed ears sprouting from each side of their head but he possessed greater strength in mind and body. Gilroy was considerably shorter but broad-shouldered, bow-legged, long-armed, and altogether a most ridiculous comical ruffian. Although Waldobert's body was slightly bent over like Gilroy's, he did not have a huge protruding stomach filled with gas and he was not afflicted with unsightly growths all over his face and body.

As he peered into the large mirror, he could see his blood shot eyes becoming clearer as the elixir began to cleanse and renew his whole system. He had become addicted to the power of the enchanted alchemy which enabled him to transform himself into any form he so wished but the constant misuse and overuse of it was slowly and surely damaging his body beyond repair. He had refused to acknowledge to himself that he was at risk of developing a permanently crouched gait because of the overuse of the serum, a condition that would progressively worsen over time, decreasing his walking efficiency and most probably leading to irreversible joint degeneration.

He stood tall now and swung his heavy black cloak around his shoulders, walked over to the door and after locking it, marched along the secret passage way.

He needed to eat a fresh chunky piece of juicy steak washed down with some fine ale that his manservant kept cooled at all times for him. After a hearty meal, he would go to see his female guests to check that they were as comfortable as expected in the circumstances and he would then need to sleep for a number of hours to regain his full strength after such time he could then deal with Gilroy and Gruntle; but for now though, he was confident that they were well locked up and were no threat to him.

When he reached the kitchen area, his manservant was preparing a thick broth for him as a starter and as he seated himself at the great wooden table, a jug of good ale was immediately placed in front of him, which he guzzled straight down; he was parched and the cool liquid went down a treat. When he had supped the thick broth full of goodness, his steak prepared just as he liked it, rare and bloody was served up in front of him.

When his appetite was fully satisfied and he had finished four jugs of ale, he felt drowsy and stood up ready to retire to his chamber for a much needed rest. As he turned from the table he suddenly lurched forward and fell to his knees grunting loudly.

Baldric rushed to his side and pulled him up and positioned him back on the chair. His head dropped forward and he seemed to lose consciousness for a few seconds but then shook his head angrily lashing out at Baldric; his countenance was deathly pale, and his looks were so wild and disordered changing from one image to another that for a few seconds Baldric shrank from him aghast.

'Leave me – I just can't think straight with you hovering over me,' he growled as he tried to stand again.

Baldric went to him again offering assistance but Waldobert seemed to recoil from his touch, his eyes narrowing as he turned to look at Baldric intently.

'Is that you Baldric,' he murmured feebly, suddenly totally vulnerable and fragile. 'For a moment, I couldn't see clearly; my eyes seem to be failing me.'

'Don't worry Sir I will help you to your feet – just lean on me.'

'I am just a little tired – help me to my bedchamber and then leave me in peace,' he said now leaning heavily on Baldric as he lifted him from the chair.

'See that our guests in the dungeons are well fed this evening and serve them all that they request – it may be their last meal.'

'I regret that I will not be able to look in on the ladies this evening but ensure that they are also comfortable and serve them whatever they ask for. I will attend to them tomorrow. I have a busy day tomorrow and need to finalise my dealings with certain undesirables and get my affairs in order so do not disturb me this night. Be sure to bring me my breakfast first thing tomorrow morning and the strongest coffee that you can prepare. And, also take this key and bring me one small vial from the locked cupboard in my laboratory.'

It appeared that he had been infused with a smidgeon of Dargo's own kindness during the frequent changes and even as he spoke, the image of Dargo's features quickly flashed across his own cruel face.

Baldric nodded as he took the key and bowed as he left his Master reclined on a couch in his bedchamber and returned to the kitchen. He was surprised that his Master had actually given him the key to his secret lair; he had never asked him to go there although Baldric knew exactly where it was. He began preparing a tray full of food left by the old cook for the female guests as instructed by his master and carefully selected some cold meats, bread, cheese, some fruit and a bottle of wine.

He strode through the dark passageway towards the wing where Claudette and Drasilla were kept captive. He knocked loudly on the door before unlocking it and entering.

Both Claudette and Drasilla sat huddled together in front of the great roaring fire. The castle was a gigantic dank, cold and draughty building and sometimes the roar of strong winds could be heard whistling along the dark chilly passageways. They both stood up when he entered; they were not so afraid of Baldric as they had at first as he had proven to be a polite and obliging manservant to them both.

Baldric placed the tray on a long table at the side of the room and began to serve up the food on various dishes for them to help themselves. He poured the wine in elaborate glasses for them as they both seated themselves.

'The master asked me to tell you that he is unable to come by to see you both this evening; he has had a very busy day but he will be sure to call in to see you tomorrow. I will be back a little later to collect the tray and I will bring you some coffee before I retire for the night myself,' he said before closing the door.

'Thank you Baldric – you're so kind to us and we do appreciate all your consideration,' Drasilla called out before the door clicked shut. They waited until they heard the key turn in the keyhole to lock the door before jumping up from their chairs to listen at the door for Baldric's retreating footsteps.

He noticed that they both seem resigned and composed in their situation, quietly chatting together, seemingly enjoying the wine and food.

When they could no longer hear his footsteps and were sure that he had left the wing, Drasilla ran over to a huge wooden armoire at the far end of the room.

'You can come out now Claude; come join us in our meal. Baldric will be back a little later with some coffee and then we can put our plan into action,' she said as Claude stepped out of the armoire.

'We have no time to lose and we must be ready tomorrow. I am hoping that Bogey has been able to alert Errol and this very day they are on their way here. I fear that another day or more will prove fatal to Dargo; he is fast losing his strength but I pray that he will be able to survive. But for now I have to resume following Baldric this evening – I suspect he will lead me straight to the Master's lair.

Chapter Thirty

Gilroy shuffled slowly around the vast dungeon area, not knowing what he was looking for but hoping for a secret opening to another passageway leading to a way out, until he came upon a partially concealed heavy wooden door at the far end. He brushed away great gnarled spider webs knitted across the door and firmly took hold of the wrought iron ring, pulling with all his strength. He slowly turned the ring which creaked loudly and pulled as hard as he could but was unable to move the door even a fraction of an inch. He gritted his teeth straining as hard as he could trying to wrench open the door.

'Don't just stand there Gruntle,' he yelled across the dungeon still grappling with the great wooden door, 'come over here and help me open this door.'

Gruntle quickly ambled over and together they pulled at the door as hard as they could; Gilroy placed one foot against the door and pulled at the door-ring with all his force but still the door would not budge an inch.

'Get behind me, put your arms around my waist and pull me,' Gilroy spluttered, his breathing becoming more laboured with the sheer exertion.

'And put a little bit of effort into it will ya,' he grunted through gritted teeth. *Sometimes I think he is as thick as a whale omelette with a peanut for a brain,* he thought to himself.

'I heard that – there is no need to be rude, you ghoulish looking simpleton; you have the wit and the sophistication of a donkey and are about as clever as a pig in a pigs swill with a sweaty ass with dew drops,' he barked back indignantly.

'Oh my, we are full of flowery compliments, aren't we,' Gilroy said snarling but tittering under his breath at the same time.

'Get stuffed,' Gruntle replied breathlessly.

'That's fine eloquent talk coming from a great respected and honourable Wizard,' Gilroy scoffed.

'When we get out of here – if we do, I'm going to see to it that you are locked up forever,' Gruntle said wheezing.

'Now you know you don't mean that,' Gilroy replied winking at him.

They both strained and heaved as hard as they could, exerting great physical effort in concentrated rhythmic bursts of strength laboriously until the door slowly began to creak open and when they had pulled it to a point where Gilroy could squeeze himself into the other side, he then began to push it open from the other side while Gruntle still pulled. Finally together they managed to open the door wide enough for Gruntle to squeeze through where they came upon a long narrow passageway.

Panting and spluttering from sheer exhaustion, Gilroy turned to peer into the darkness and suddenly stepped back startled, placing one hand over his nose to dispel the overpowering pungent odour coming from within; the stench was incredibly nauseating, filling his nostrils with putrid aromas of rotting flesh, assaulting the sensitive membranes of his nose; it smelt like a multitude of rats had been drowned and left to rot in sewage.

As they walked a few paces further along the narrow passageway, they came to a narrow iron door with bars, by the side of which hung a large iron key which Gilroy inserted into the centre of a massive lock. As the key was turned, the bolts of the great lock moved loudly and the iron door swung open.

As Gilroy's eyes became accustomed to the darkness of the dungeon, he was overcome with terror as he sank back barely able to breathe at the horror he was seeing before him. He sank to his knees horrified inches away from the mutilated remains of small bodies with little battered wings strewn around the room. The windows were cast with thick iron bars and there was hardly any lighting in the dungeon, or in the passage adjoining it. No one could have possibly been able to escape from this prison of oppressive hell.

He dragged himself up from the ground and staggered around hardly able to believe what he was seeing. In one corner of the dungeon he could see the figure of a woman and child huddled close together and he knew instinctively that it was Petra and Gilda. He rushed over to them and covered their poor mutilated bodies as much as he could with the heap of ragged clothing nearby to them.

'Poor Dargo – this will devastate him and may be the end of him now,' he uttered in a strangled whisper.

'What is it?' Gruntle asked. On seeing the expression on Gilroy's face, he clutched at his heart.

'I'm afraid it's the very worst news for Dargo,' Gilroy answered crossing himself.

'Help us – help us!' Gruntle then screamed as he stared at the mangled heap of flesh before them with unutterable anguish on his face.

'Be quiet,' Gilroy hissed as he turned and slapped Gruntle's face to calm him.

'We are dealing with a foul monster beyond our worst imagination,' he added shuddering.

As they stood there breathing laboriously, Gilroy felt that he would never be able to free his mind from the memory of the dreadful appalling image of that horrible charnel pit, which seemed to go down to the very bowels of hell. They quickly retreated back out of the narrow grated iron door, locking it behind them and groping their way back to the dungeon where Waldobert had left them.

Chapter Thirty-One

Claude had found it relatively easy in the circumstances to pass himself off as Baldric to enable him to track down the wing where Drasilla and Claudette were being kept. He had been able to snatch a uniform from Baldric's bedchamber which gave him the freedom to wander around the fortress without causing any suspicion from the old cook or the other servants.

With the help of the Master's coarse mouthed cook-housekeeper, who was a distorted warped looking old man with a dull complexion, a long hooked nose and a chin covered with blotches, the result of habitual intemperance, he was also able to acquire a set of spare keys to all the doors in the great castle.

It had not only been amazingly easy to fool the old cook but it had been almost entertaining for Claude although he realized that it was not a time or place for his light entertainment, he nevertheless could not help being amused by the old cook and his obvious befuddlement at times.

He had watched the movements of the Master closely during the last two days and had been able to form his plan of action. He made his way back to the lair, having followed Baldric earlier and while the Master was sleeping now took one of the vast number of vials of elixir. These small phials were stocked in drawers adjacent to rows and rows of small glass casements each containing a tiny blue fairy, their small faces staring at him as if imploring him to set them free. The lair almost lit up with the glow of the huge collection of blue fairies entrapped and imprisoned in the glass casements. He could hear their tiny tinkling cries for help as they pressed their faces up against the glass containers.

Claude was horrified when he realized that this was the Master's great laboratory where his magical elixir was prepared extracting the magical blood from the blue fairies.

Claude was relieved that they had at last found the collection of lost blue fairies and he promised himself that he would come back and release them all when it was all over.

'Do not worry little ones, I will be back to set you free,' he mouthed at them silently and turned from them not wanting them to see him with one of the phials and what he was about to do with it.

He had observed the effects of the magical substance on Waldobert's body, giving him incredible strength and Claude knew that in order to defeat him, he would need that same strength to fight him as an equal. He held up the sparkling liquid and without a second thought of any possible disastrous consequences to himself drank it down quickly.

He laid himself down while the liquid began its magic on his body. Unlike the effect it had on Waldobert of completely changing his form, there was a gradual rush of incredible energy through his veins and his body started to pulsate with strength. When the whole process had completed, he stood tall and strong after being invigorated by the magic stimulant.

Claude left the laboratory and hastily began descending the stairs when suddenly he heard a loud roar resounding through the passage way and thundering footsteps were heard approaching the stairway, at the foot of which he found Waldobert waiting grasping a mallet with a deadly and determined expression on his face. He sprang halfway up the stairway howling like a demented raging rampant wolf, his eyes blazing like two fireballs.

He flew at Claude wielding the mallet menacingly, but then tossing it away down the stairs as he made a grab for Claude, his hands clutching at his neck as he lifted him into the air like a rag doll, his body thrashing around like a trapped animal.

They were elevated above the stairway like two horrific oversized bats locked in fierce combat. Waldobert's demonic laughter rang out and echoed through the Fortress.

'You poor demented fool, you cannot fight me – I am the all consuming power that you cannot possibly defeat,' he screamed at Claude.

'You vile despicable monster,' Claude bellowed at the top of his voice. 'I will squeeze every ounce of life out of your body, just like you drained every drop of blood from all those poor little wretches that you have collected and feasted on all these years.'

With his newfound mighty strength Claude was able to wrench himself free from

Waldobert's steely grasp around his neck and throw a punch which slammed into Waldobert's middle; Waldobert was propelled back spinning in the air, winded for a second or two but then hurled himself once again at Claude throwing several blows to his face and body.

They continued grappling in the air but after a violent struggle when Waldobert had grasped Claude's head in a powerful arm-hold, Waldobert's body suddenly seemed to seize up and losing his grip on Claude's head, he plummeted down onto the stairway and tumbled down the remainder of the stairs.

He lay there momentarily stunned but then stirred and shook his head roaring like a lion. His eyes blazed as he looked up at Claude before rolling over and suddenly leaping up from the ground and sprinting off along the passageway with a sudden burst of renewed energy towards his lair.

Claude lowered himself down and quickly ran down the stairway, picked up the mallet and blundered after him. He knew he had no time to lose and had to reach him before he was able to restore his strength with another vial of elixir.

He chased him until he reached Waldobert's lair but not before Waldobert was able to slam the door and lock it. He heard Waldobert's demonic laughter from within. He stood back and lashing out with the mallet pounded continually on the massive wrought iron lock until after some considerable time broke it and the door flew open.

He peered into the room but Waldobert was nowhere to be seen; he cautiously stepped into the lair and stood quickly scanning the room from corner to corner before walking across to another door at the far end of the lair, when he uttered a cry of pain as he stepped onto some broken glass. As he leaned over and picked up the broken phial, he knew that Waldobert had probably changed his form again but he could not now be sure what form he had taken on.

Claude had told Drasilla and Claudette that he would come back to their room at lunch time to prepare them for their escape but when there had been no sign of his return, they had begun to feel fraught with anxiety. Drasilla knew that Claude would have also alerted Gilroy and Gruntle to his plan of escape, but she could not see how they could possibly overpower Waldobert. His strength was that of twenty men and Claude with his bent gait, Gilroy with his stumpy overweight form, and, well, Gruntle was after all just a feeble old man; together they had no chance of defeating Waldobert.

'What do you think has happened Drasilla, do you think something bad has happened to Claude? Maybe we should just go on ahead and try to find our way out of here,' Claudette said as she anxiously wrung her hands together continually marching back and forth across the room.

'Yes, I'm sure something has happened. Baldric normally checks on us at this time of the day and where is he? Not that we want him to check on us because when he finds the door unlocked, he will know for sure that something is going on,' Drasilla replied now also wringing her hands in extreme agitation.

'It is just so quiet, even the rats and bats are nowhere to be seen today; they all scuttled back into all the crevices in the walls – it's as if they know something bad is coming,' Claudette said, her brow wrinkling with worry.

Drasilla quickly walked over to Claudette to comfort her and as she put her arms around her shoulders, Claudette laid her head on her shoulders as she began to weep.

'Shush my dear, please don't cry, I am confident that between them, they will find a way to get us out of here,' she told her, desperately trying to convince herself.

'But how are they going to get Dargo out of here when he has lost all his strength – he has been robbed of his mighty wings,' Claudette said sobbing still.

Claude had explained the grisly situation to them and that Dargo himself was also being held captive deep down in the darkest dungeons and was gravely wounded. They had both cried out in shock when he told them that his powerful wings had been ripped from his body rendering him completely helpless and under the mercy of Waldobert, Gilroy's evil twin, the Troll Warrior.

They had both been astounded that they had been fooled by the evil Troll Warrior masquerading himself as Dargo. Claudette had begun to weep uncontrollably.

'Come now Claudette, we just have to have a bit of trust; you know how cunning Gilroy is – I just know he will find a way – we must have faith, no matter how little,' Drasilla had replied stroking Claudette's forehead to soothe her.

After some time waiting patiently and becoming more and more anxious by the hour, Drasilla and Claudette decided to make a move and after checking outside that there was no sign of Baldric or the Master, cautiously stepped out into the dark passageway.

They nervously made their way along the long draughty passageway holding hands. Claudette's body shook violently as she walked a little behind as Drasilla guided her along.

They both stopped abruptly when they came face to face with Baldric; Drasilla immediately clasped Claudette closer to her as they stood looking at Baldric.

'Madam, you must go back to your quarters immediately. The Master is on the rampage and I must insist, for your own safety, that you go back now.

Claudette's eyes widened with fear as a demonic roar echoed throughout the passageway and they could hear doors being violently slammed.

'What has happened Baldric – is your Master ill?' Drasilla asked him.

'Yes Madam, I fear very much that he is extremely sick and his mood is quite violent this day. You must return back to your cell for your own safety and please do not make a sound. He has had these episodes of extreme rage before and we have to wait until it subsides,' Baldric replied as he gently pushed them in front, guiding them quickly back to their quarters.

'But Baldric, please tell us what is going on. We are both so worried about Dargo and we fear that he is growing weaker as time goes on.'

'Why would you feel worried about Dargo and what do you mean that he is growing weaker – who told you this? You have seen for yourself that he is well and strong. He is just angry this day and as I told you he frequently has episodes of explosive moods,' he replied appearing puzzled.

'I just have an awful sense of his pain Baldric; I just know that he has been badly wounded. How else could Waldobert sustain so much power and maintain his image for long periods of time.'

'I don't know what you are saying Madam, Dargo is my Master and I don't know who this Waldobert is.'

'You know perfectly well that Waldobert is your Master; he is just parading himself off as Dargo – I am just losing my patience with you now Baldric,' she replied angrily.

'As I have just told you Madam, stay here and be very, very quiet. If the Master hears that you tried to escape, he will become more violent and I dread to think what he will do to you both.'

Both Drasilla and Claudette nodded shrinking back as he slammed the heavy door shut and locked it; the room almost shuddering at the impact. They gasped startled as the small metal flap in the middle of the door then suddenly flipped open and two red blazing eyes peered inside at them.

'Did you think you could get away that easy – you will pay for that,' the voice from the other side bellowed.

They both reared back in horror as they heard the loud demonic laughter again and then the sound of heavy pounding footsteps thundering away along the passageway.

Chapter Thirty-Two

Claude climbed stealthily down the stone stairway, frequently turning to look over his shoulder to assure himself that he was not being followed. He needed to alert both Gilroy and Gruntle to the situation; they would now need to stay together and wait for the right time to overwhelm Waldobert again; they would need to wait until he slept this night.

Claude clung to a set of iron keys that clattered in his hand as he made his way down the steps. The keys would release Dargo from the heavy iron chains that imprisoned him cruelly leaving him helpless to move.

'Is that you Baldric,' he heard Gilroy whisper in a darkened corner of the dungeon.

'It's OK Gilroy, it's me,' Claude replied. 'We have to be careful, I thought I had defeated Waldobert but he got away before the full extent of his magic elixir had worn off but he has been alerted now to danger. We will have to wait until he is sleeping this evening but we can't be sure where he will hide to rest himself.'

'But for now let's rest awhile ourselves and have some broth that the old cook has prepared. Baldric is on his way down with the food and we can prepare ourselves for what we have to do this coming night.'

Much later when they had all rested and were feeling stronger after supping the broth, they began preparing themselves for the inevitable battle with Waldobert.

During their tour of the dungeons located in the lower part of the castle accessed through dimly lit winding passages leading from their own cell, many of them left unlocked, they had found a torture chamber full of instruments and devices especially designed to inflict unbearable pain and suffering on an unfortunate victim. They each clasped a heavy weapon that they had picked up from that torture chamber in readiness to defend themselves. Both Gilroy and Gruntle held a heavy ball and chain and Claude clutched an iron mallet.

As they now drew nearer to Waldobert's chamber clutching their combat weapon, creeping silently along until they reached the thick wooden studded door, they paused for a moment each filled with horror and dread before opening it. Gilroy's hand trembled uncontrollably as he turned the iron doorknob ring which creaked loudly as it turned and the door swung open; they cringed as they stepped inside the great ominous chamber as they immediately felt the supreme evil in the blackness of the chamber.

As they advanced stepping stealthily forward nearer to his wooden sleeping tomb they shuddered as they could see that the top of the crypt was slightly ajar and a strange green light swirled from within. They trembled numb with fear as they crept even more closely until they were able to lean over on tiptoe and peer inside where they could see Waldobert grunting and groaning, his teeth grinding as he slept fitfully.

Gruntle suddenly gasped as he crossed himself and dropped to his knees in silent prayer. His lips moving rapidly as he mutely spoke the words of his garbled prayer, repeating his nervous jumbled words over and over again until his prayer was interrupted by a swift kick up his backside by Gilroy.

'Would you get up and stop acting like the village idiot,' Gilroy hissed through his teeth, dragging him up by the scruff of his neck. 'We've no time to lose here and we must act quickly before he smells us. And, this is no time for jokes – I know what you are going to say,' he quickly added pointing his finger with great conviction and emphasis at Gruntle as he started to open his mouth to reply.

'I was only going to say that ... Oh never mind what I was going to say,' Gruntle in turn hissed through his teeth.

'Yes, I know exactly what you were going to say ... You always have to insult me, don't you! I can't help the way I smell.'

'Just you remember my boy that I am your elder and you should have respect for your elders,' he replied now wagging his finger in Gilroy's face.

'I don't believe you two actually standing here bickering at a time like this,' Claude hissed. 'You are like two grumpy old men continually complaining and squabbling.'

'Well, he started it,' Gilroy grunted.

'No, you started it,' Gruntle snapped back.

'Shush you two, you will wake him,' whispered Claude.

'What a gruesome 'orrible sight,' Gilroy in turn whispered as he now gazed down at Waldobert's face in the midst of the swirling green substance.

'Yes, a regular sleeping beauty isn't he. He's out for the count,' Gruntle said as he raised his ball on a chain high above his head ready to swing it. 'I just want to knock his block off right now.'

'Be careful with that thing will ya, you could do some serious damage with that,' Gilroy hissed.

'Yes well, that's the idea,' Gruntle replied as he began swinging the ball faster around his head until it began whirring loudly.

But as the ball began to swing around precariously, Gruntle lost his balance and grip on the chain sending the ball spinning across the other side of the room and then crashing loudly against the thick brick wall.

'You moron, now he's sure to have heard that,' Gilroy hissed through his teeth.

Waldobert suddenly stirred and his eyes snapped wide open like two burning fire balls erupting from his head. He sat bolt upright, roaring like a demented demon.

'WHO DARES TO DISTURB ME IN MY SLEEP,' he bellowed as he leapt out of his crypt.

Startled and frozen with fear to the point that they could hardly move; their legs becoming almost immobile, Gilroy, Gruntle and Claude immediately shrank down on their knees and crawled around the other side of the wooden box pitifully, desperately trying to hide from the fiend that they had awakened.

When Waldobert hovered over them like a giant demon roaring like a lion with a toothache, they seemed to conjure up enough strength from where they knew not, sprung up from the side of the wooden coffin like three deranged frogs and dashed out of the chamber along the dark passageway.

They could hear the demonic howling echoing through the castle walls as they ran as fast as their legs could carry them. Waldobert thundered after them all the while cursing them.

'You cannot escape me you heap of dung, you bag of putrid rotten worms full of pus; I will find you and when I do, I will stamp on you and crush you until you are nothing but dust under my feet.'

'Oh that's charming, I think he's really mad now,' Gilroy spluttered hardly able to breathe as they ran.

'Would you just SHUT UP,' Claude replied sharply equally out of breathe.

They fled through the winding passages, never stopping to even glance over their shoulders until they were exhausted and could run no more.

'I have to rest,' Gruntle spluttered. 'I am but an old man and my legs cannot move another inch,' he cried as he staggered and slumped to the ground breathing laboriously.

'OK, we can rest now; the castle is vast and through these endless winding tunnels and passageways how can Waldobert possibly find us,' Gilroy gasped panting for air.

'Don't be fooled for one minute, he can find us anywhere,' Claude said as he slumped down beside Gruntle.

'I am so hungry, I've not eaten since supper time,' Gilroy announced rubbing his stomach. I need some sustenance before I can even think straight.'

'This is no time to think of your stomach Gilroy,' Gruntle grumbled. 'Besides, you have enough fat in your body to last for at least a year,' he added smirking.

'Now there you go again, I've just about had enough of your insults Gruntle. Can't you ever think of saying something nice to me without splurging out verbal diarrhoea to hurt my feelings?'

'Quiet you two,' Claude said suddenly alert to footsteps clattering along nearby to them.

They clung to each other unable to move as the clattering footsteps got closer and closer.

'Just a minute,' Gilroy suddenly announced, 'I know that perfume and those footsteps can only mean that the person coming towards us is wearing high heels.'

Claude then raised his face frantically sniffing at the air. 'Yes, you are right, that smell of musk and sandalwood can only belong to Drasilla.'

'I had no idea you knew so much about perfume,' Gilroy said looking impressed.

'Just shut it,' Claude replied impatiently. 'It may surprise you to learn that I know much more than you could ever imagine.'

'Oh now you are showing off Claude – just because you have established yourself as the leader of this little escapade that we have found ourselves in you suddenly imagine that you are an expert of women's perfume.'

'I... I just cannot believe this – here we are running for our very lives and you stand there full of jealousy and mocking my every move. I tell you, I am sick and tired of it,' Claude replied indignantly.

'Oooh, we are precious all of a sudden, aren't we,' Gilroy said mockingly.

They both turned as Gruntle had placed one hand on each of their shoulders and began roughly shaking them.

'He is almost upon us,' he uttered almost too softly to be heard but they both immediately quietened their bickering, their mouths agape and their eyes wide open in horror. Gruntle began crossing himself and babbling in his prayer again.

Chapter Thirty-Three

As Gilroy and Gruntle stood behind Claude, now both clutching onto his arms, they drew back as the clattering footsteps were now getting closer and closer. They could also now hear the swishing of a gown as the footsteps were now almost upon them and the smell of the perfume became even more pungent.

'Don't make a sound,' Gilroy whispered as he drew them both down until they were on their knees.

He then clamped his hand over Gruntle's mouth as his teeth began chattering loudly.

'Pull yourself together man,' Gilroy hissed at him.

They drew their breath in sharply as Drasilla suddenly appeared before them, out of breath and panting profusely, frantically fanning herself with her sequined fan.

'Oh my darling boys, am I so very ever so glad to see you. You boys can certainly make a girl run for her money,' she gushed giggling and gasping for breath, her hand on her heaving chest.

'Oh our very own darling girl, are we ever so pleased to see you! What are you doing up and about in the dead of the night like this?' Gilroy replied.

'I'm looking for you boys of course. Claudette and I have been waiting patiently the whole day for you all to rescue us and when you didn't turn up, I decided to come looking for you,' she replied fluttering her eyelids wildly at them.

Both Claude and Gruntle stood back quietly although puzzled by Drasilla's seemingly peculiar behaviour.

In all the time that Claude had known her, Drasilla had never been one to flutter her eyelids or behave in such a dizzy ditzy way.

'Well we've certainly had a hard time and this very night we tried to capture Waldobert while he was at his most vulnerable, resting in his crypt but he was immediately alerted to our presence and flew out after us like a bat out of hell,' Gilroy explained. 'And we can thank Gruntle for that; he's like a bull in a china shop fumbling around like an idiot; completely lacking in any kind of skill or grace – awkward, gauche, inept, you name it.'

'Like a bat out of hell and a bull in a china shop, why that is so funny Gilroy – you are such a ridiculous clown sometimes,' Drasilla said beginning to giggle uncontrollably and then laughing raucously.

Claude turned to look at Gilroy raising one eyebrow, now completely suspicious of her bizarre behaviour especially as when she hauled up her gown as she walked nearer to them, he noticed that her ankles were extremely hairy.

'You poor dear damsel in distress, I think you are a tad bit hysterical Drasilla; have you been drinking?' Gilroy then asked as he put his arm around her shoulders patting her affectionately on her back.

'Poor demented damsel in distress, more likely,' Gruntle muttered under his breath. He was beginning to become more uneasy by the minute as she stood before them behaving most unlike her normal level-headed self.

'Yes, I think I am boys,' she replied as she hung her head, her voice suddenly becoming husky as she coughed nervously to clear her throat.

'Sit awhile and rest while you catch your breath my dear,' Gilroy told her also feeling disturbed by her unbecoming erratic manner.

'Let's just get back to Claudette; she must be so frightened on her own. We then can rest up for a while and decide what we are going to do. I have so many questions that I need to ask you,' she replied as she mopped her brow with the end of her gown.

Gruntle gasped as he could now see that the rest of her legs were certainly very hairy.

'Never mind about questions Drasilla; we've no time to waste standing around answering your questions. What's come over you – we just want to get the hellabaloo out of here,' Gilroy said completely exasperated by her blasé behaviour.

'But I thought you wanted me to rest up here for a while,' Drasilla spluttered suddenly bursting into tears.

'Oh forgive me my dear, I didn't mean to upset you – it's just that we are all nervous and anxious to get out of here.'

'Oh for God's sake would you stop that blabbering Drasilla, you are getting on my nerves,' Gruntle muttered as he roughly rubbed at his beard hardly able to contain his ill-temper.

'Please don't talk to me like that, I don't deserve that. You are being most unkind and disrespectful and I won't forget that Gruntle,' she said sniffing, still dabbing her face with the hem of her gown.

'Apologise right now,' Gilroy demanded angrily. 'You have no right to speak to Drasilla like that.'

'OK, I apologise Drasilla. Can we go now,' he said sighing impatiently.

'I am not very impressed with your apology or the tone of your voice,' Drasilla replied indignantly.

'Oh for God's sake – let's get going now,' Gilroy growled as he put one arm around Drasilla's shoulder again guiding her forward.

Gilroy led her on while Gruntle and Claude followed somewhat half-heartedly as they slowly but quietly crept back up to the second level where Claudette was waiting for them.

As they arrived at the doorway fraught with anxiety, they rushed through the open door to find both Drasilla and Claudette sat on chairs back to back tied securely with thick rope. They gasped as their heads spun round to look at the form standing behind them.

'Yes you fools, it is but I, your very own sweet damsel in distress,' Waldobert said fluttering his eyelashes at them again as he threw back his head laughing out loudly.

'Oh this is such a grand game that I play – it never fails me,' he added smugly.

'I knew it – I just took one look at your hairy legs and I knew you couldn't possibly be Drasilla,' Gruntle grunted.

'Why didn't you say something?' Gilroy now asked him.

Gruntle stood looking at them dumfounded.

'I can't believe that you didn't notice his legs – you must be blind or stupid, you great overgrown slug with legs,' Gruntle finally said spluttering.

'Right, that does it – I told you I am sick and tired of your insults,' Gilroy said as he lurched himself at Gruntle.

Waldobert quickly took hold of Gilroy, his thick arm now grasping him around his neck nearly choking him.

'Now, now boys, let's not fight amongst yourselves; you need to keep up your strength for your future survival such as it is,' Waldobert scoffed.

'Steady on yer lord-ship, you are choking the life out of me,' Gilroy rasped; his legs now floundering desperately trying to regain his balance as he was roughly lifted off the ground.

'Oh God, we've been fooled yet again,' Gilroy croaked spluttering as he struggled to breathe. 'Could you just loosen the arm-hold just a tad bit my good Sir,' he continued trying to appear nonchalant and as calm as he could.

'SHUT IT,' Waldobert growled as he then booted both Gruntle and Claude further into the room, sending them sprawling onto the ground at the feet of Drasilla and Claudette; he then backed out of the door still holding onto Gilroy firmly around his neck, kicked the door closed and locked the door securely behind him.

Gruntle dropped to his knees and began pounding his fists on the hard ground. 'This is beginning to feel like one of those nightmares where you go round and around and going nowhere – will we ever be able to get out of this place.'

'Are you OK?' Claude asked Drasilla and Claudette as he stood up dusting himself down and sneezing repeatedly.

'To think I nearly kissed him on first seeing him disguised as Drasilla,' Gruntle said shuddering as he too stood up. 'Now what are we going to do?'

'Well I'll tell you what we are going to do,' replied Claude looking smug all of a sudden. 'I've got spare keys to all the cells and we are going to get out of here sooner than you think. Now let's untie you two girls.'

'I don't think it is going to be that easy,' Drasilla said turning to look at a closet slightly rocking on the other side where a muffled sound could be heard.

'Claude ran over to the closet and inside, also tied up was his brother Baldric.

'I'm so sorry Claude; the Master caught me trying to help the girls escape and shut me in here – he took all my keys from me and the copies that you had stored inside this closet.'

'Oh God help us, we are never going to escape now,' Gruntle began wailing as he threw his arms around Claudette and the chair she was tied to.

'Pull yourself together Pappy and be quiet, we have to think and we can't think while you are making so much noise,' Claudette said. 'And could you now untie us please.'

Gruntle quickly straightened up looking sheepish. 'Yes my darling little girl, I am so sorry behaving like a wimp and you remaining so brave and eloquent.

Chapter Thirty-Four

Gilroy struggled frantically as Waldobert dragged him along the dark passageway and down to the lower dungeons where he tossed him into one of the open cells. Gilroy was sent hurtling across the cold stone flooring and before he could recover his balance, he felt a blow to the back of his head and his senses began to reel, spinning into complete blackness.

Waldobert slammed the heavy cell door shut and locked it securely, laughing as he then tossed the key along the dark passageway where it fell through a grated opening.

'That's the end of him and his meddling and interfering into my business – he will never get out of there now. Two gone and one to go and I can't wait to stop that Sheriff in his tracks. I will show them all who is the

Master,' he muttered as he began to make his way through the secret passageways leading back to his lair and laboratory.

He started to call out for Baldric but then he remembered that he had earlier that day locked him in the lower quarters with Drasilla and Claudette.

'A person just can't find decent staff these days,' he muttered.

As he strode through the long passageway, his vision began to get blurred; he felt strange and he began to sweat profusely. He knew that his body was beginning to shut down again and he could do nothing about it; the serum was malfunctioning in his system again. He no longer had any control over the transformation course now and as he felt himself becoming weaker and weaker he began to drag his feet along; they felt heavy like huge stumps of wood; he stumbled forward as if intoxicated and then finally fell to the ground with a thud.

He lay there in the darkness for some time until he slowly regained consciousness. He awoke to find the old cook standing over him attempting to haul him onto his feet.

'Are you OK Madam – what are you doing here,' he heard the old cook say. 'I'll need to help you get back to your quarters;

if the Master catches you like this, he will not be pleased.'

'No, no you drunken old fool, I am your Master. Help me up at once – I need to get back to my lair immediately,' he ordered.

The old cook struggled and strained to help him back on his feet but could not lift him.

'Oh dear, oh dear,' the old cook muttered under his breath. 'What am I to do with you?' He had been drinking quite heavily as usual and as much as he tried to heave the seemingly heavy woman onto her feet, he knew that he did not have the strength to move her by himself.

'How could such a delicate creature be so heavy,' he moaned to himself as he lost his grip and Waldobert slid back on the hard ground. All the strenuous back-breaking heaving had left him shattered; he was worn out and flopped down next to Waldobert breathing heavily – he needed to rest for a few minutes to catch his breath.

After several minutes had gone by, he then mustered up all the strength he could in the circumstance, heaved himself up from the cold ground and hurriedly made his way down to the lower quarters for help. When he arrived at the cell where Drasilla and Claudette were being held, he fumbled clumsily, dropping the key several times before unlocking the door and then stood there swaying and panting in his drunken state, surprised when he found himself face to face with Claude and Gruntle.

'Is that you Baldric?' he asked hesitantly peering at them both, his eyes narrowing hardly able to focus on their faces. The ground beneath his feet seemed to be swaying and he felt as if he was going to vomit.

He suddenly gasped as Baldric stepped out of the shadows and stood next to Claude. He strained his neck out to focus on them as the image of them both began to spin before his eyes.

'I'm seeing double,' he groaned rubbing his eyes as he turned to flee, but before he had a chance to scuttle off, Claude had, as quick as lightning, rushed at him and holding onto him firmly dragged him through to the room and just as quickly snatched the keys from his hand.

'What's going on here,' the old cook cried as Claude then quickly pushed him onto a chair.

'Quick Drasilla, hand me that rope over there; we need to tie him up and put him in that cupboard over there.'

'Tie me up ... you can't do that to me; I need to prepare lunch for the Master.'

'Sorry about this – we don't mean to harm you,' Claude told him.

Drasilla grabbed the rope and handed it to Claude who quickly tied the old cook to the chair making sure that his hands and legs were securely bound.

'This is despicable and yer all will pay for this – wait 'til the Master comes down! He will sort the lot of you out and good riddance to yer all – tricking an old man like this. Yer all should be ashamed of yerselves,' he continued spluttering and panting.

He then sat peering crossed-eyed at Drasilla and her image also began to spin around and around before his eyes before he toppled, chair and all sideways onto the floor.

Now I am seeing double again – I must give up the drink, he thought as he hung his head averting his eyes from her.

Claude quickly hauled him back up. 'Just sit there quietly will you and the less you wriggle around on the chair, the better for you.'

'How did you get back here so soon anyway? Why, I just left you slumped along the secret passageway trying to get into the Master's lair,' the old cook mumbled almost incoherently looking at Drasilla. 'And may I ask what were you doing outside the Master's lair Madam,' he continued staring at her suspiciously.

'What is he babbling on about?' Gruntle asked. 'We are wasting our time standing around here listening to this drunken sod.'

'It's all a trick – you are all trying to trick me,' the old cook continued muttering to himself. 'Just you wait till I tell the Master about you all – he will not be very pleased at all.

She turned to look at Claude puzzled. 'What did he say – what is he talking about Claude?'

'I think he has just seen Waldobert masquerading as you – he is confused.'

'Well, he's not the only one – I can tell you that,' Gruntle complained. 'All this masked cloak and dagger business and masquerading around as someone else is giving me a headache.'

Claude stood over the old cook and gently slapped his face to keep him from dropping off into a drunken slumber. 'So where is "Madam" now?' he asked him.

'Pleash yer honour, I didn't done nuffin honest!' he spluttered as he shook his head from side to side trying to avoid eye contact with Claude.

'What did you do with Madam – where did you leave her?' Claude asked again.

'OK, OK, she is sleeping outside the Master's lair,' he replied drooling as saliva began to trickle down his chin. 'Me thinks she has been drinking and is the worse for wear but I didn't do nuffin to her I swear – I was jush trying to help.' He grunted again and then his head slumped forward and he was out for the count.

'Quick Gruntle,' Claude continued, 'We need to get to Waldobert before he awakens. This is our chance to overcome him – you stay here,' he said turning to Drasilla and Claudette. 'You come with us,' he then said turning to Baldric.

'Can't I just stay here as well,' Gruntle whined. 'After all the girls need protecting and I want to stay close by to Claudette.'

Claude sighed, irritated by Gruntle's constant lack of courage.

'That does make sense,' Baldric said.

'OK, you stay Gruntle but keep the door locked.'

Chapter Thirty-Five

Errol pushed open the great wrought iron gate and began walking along a winding pathway overgrown with wild and prickly foliage with Wally, all the while panting and frantically sniffing along the route, occasionally barking as he trotted along. His band of Officers and the Pug brothers were also close behind at his heels all the while trying to avoid the wild and prickly foliage that nipped at their feet and legs like tiny ferocious bulldogs.

The Pug brothers hopped along the way yelping all the while on their high heeled shoes. 'Ouch you pesky ugly little devils,' Clancy complained as he sometimes booted at the little growling and spitting faces scattered around the ground.

'Who are you calling ugly little devils – you are the ugly little devils more like it,' one of the little faces squeaked at him, poking its tongue out him.

'No, you are,' replied Clancy, in turn poking his tongue out at the small face.

'No, you are,' the tiny face repeated.

'Would you just shut it – I am surrounded by a bunch of unruly children,' Errol groaned. 'Now just get behind me and be QUIET, or else.'

'Or else what,' Clancy said as he ducked just in time to avoid Errol's hand swiping the back of his head.

'What is all this head swiping about,' he whispered to himself.

They trudged on until they came to a secret ancient thick door covered in cobwebs and long talon-like weeds winding around the doorway with tiny gargoyle faces hissing and spitting at them.

'Good we've found it at last – this is the secret entrance leading to the underground passageways of the castle,' Errol said as he began brushing away the cobwebs and hacking off the obstructing now shrieking weeds.

He turned the great brass handle and pressed his shoulder firmly against the heavy door, pushing hard until the door slowly creaked open. He beckoned the men to follow and as they all entered into the secret opening they then silently crept down a steep stone stairway leading down to the underground of the castle.

The thick walls each side of the stairway leading down to the underground were covered in green moss and as they finally descended to the lower level, they all held their breath and covered their mouth and nose with their hands as the dank stale smell hit them.

'We need to split up and search all the dungeons,' Errol said as half of his men then marched off in one direction and the rest started off in another direction.

'What about us?' the Pug brothers yelled behind him. They had become embroiled in a competition with the gargoyle faces, pulling equally ugly faces and poking out their tongues to the little creatures.

Errol turned – he had for a minute forgotten about the Pug brothers, which he now realized was a bit unfair as they had after all led them to the secret doorway even though they were unbearably irritating. 'You come with me but I want you to promise that you will be as quiet as mice; I don't want you scuttling off shrieking at the slightest little sound,' he warned them wagging his finger at them.

'Oh darling, you can be sure we will be as quiet as little tartlets,' Clancy said mincing along after Errol.

'Just follow me and be quiet – I'm warning you; one more sound and I will kick all free of you out,' Errol snarled.

Cedric and Cecil both nodded as they pushed Clancy in front as they all then followed Errol as he began striding along the dark passageway. Most of the cells were left unopened and as they trudged along the dark passageways peering into each cell they began to fear that they were too late. The vast area of the underground cells appeared to have been cleaned out and there was no sign of any person or persons ever having been imprisoned in the dungeons.

Errol and the Pug brothers seemed to come around in full circle and eventually came face to face with his other officers.

'Did you find anything?' Errol asked as they stopped in front of him.

'Nothing Sir,' his Chief Officer replied. 'All the cells appear to have been cleaned out and there is no sign of any prisoners.'

'Oh no, I fear the worst now!' Errol said as he stood there rubbing his forehead as if in pain or deep thought. 'Maybe we are too late.'

Suddenly the Pug brothers stacked themselves on top of each other so that Clancy was in line with Errol's shoulders and he began massaging his back.

'What are you doing now for God's sake,' Errol hissed through his teeth.

'Just giving you a massage – you were rubbing your forehead and that is a sign of having a headache so I thought you needed a massage,' Clancy said as he then gently patted the top of Errol's head.

'Get down this instant and get away from me,' Errol growled swiping at him with one hand so that Clancy toppled from the shoulders of Cedric who then toppled from the shoulders of Cecil.

'Oooh you brute,' Clancy cried as he lay now rubbing his own head. 'There's no need to be so ill tempered about it – we were only trying to help.'

'Yes, well you are all so irritating and I can tell you how much you GET ON MY NERVES,' he said yelling at them now at the top of his voice.

'Oh darling, is that any way to treat those poor little mites. You big bully – I am that disappointed with you darling. You just wait till I tell your wife what a big beastly bully of a brute you have become.'

Errol spun around, rushed at Drasilla and gathered her in his arms, wrapping his strong arms around her tightly.

'Drasilla, where did you spring from,' he said still clutching her firmly against his great strong chest.

'My dear, you can't begin to imagine what I've been through being kept here in these damp evil smelling dungeons. I'm positively worn out and I could just murder for a hot bath with lavender smelling salts,' she said through clenched teeth trying desperately to disentangle herself from his strong grasp.

'Yes, I see what you mean,' Errol said as he suddenly released her, his nostrils visibly twitching at the unfortunate smell emanating from her somewhat grubby appearance.

'My dear girl, you look and smell as if you have been dragged through a rat infested pit and back. But never mind we will soon have you back to all your home comforts and you will soon look your usual glamorous self.'

'Oooh darling you are awful and I love you dearly for that but more importantly let me take you to where Claudette, Gilroy and Dargo are being kept – just follow me my dears,' she said beckoning them through a wrought iron drop down gated entrance.

'Yes, the sooner we can get you all out of this depressing dismal evil smelling place, the better,' Errol said as he and his men followed her through the opening. 'Thank God we have found you – I can't tell you how worried I've been about you dear Drasilla; you've been sorely missed.'

He failed to notice the sly look on Drasilla's face as she turned back to look at him and no sooner had he spoken when she suddenly rushed back past them all through the entrance, quickly pulled a handle on the outside and the heavy wrought iron gate dropped down with a crash trapping them all inside.

'What are you doing Drasilla?' Errol asked turning to look at her through the bars, completely puzzled at her behaviour. 'Have you completely lost your senses?' he asked reaching out to grasp her hand through the bars.

But without even answering she had rushed off laughing in a strange way; her guttural loud laughter could be heard echoing through the dark passageway as she ran faster and faster away from them.

'Whatever has come over her – she's lost her mind. Been in here too long I fear,' he said scratching his head.

Chapter Thirty-Six

Claude could hear the loud guttural laughter along the passageway as he slowly crept along and before he knew it he came face to face with Drasilla. He knew without a doubt that it was Waldobert once again in the guise of Drasilla. Although the long dark hair cascading around the slender shoulders and the near perfect bone structure was clear to be seen, Claude could see a slight dark hair growth beginning around the jaw line and the legendary violet eyes were blood shot and sinister.

'Help me Claude my darling man, I've been attacked by Waldobert and he has been chasing me all around the dungeons,' he said in a croaky voice, clearing his throat loudly.

'You've just about used up all your masquerading trickery Waldobert and you are not fooling any of us now, so let's get this over with once and for all.'

'Oh so we think we are so clever do we? But you don't stand a chance against me, you little weak nondescript excuse for a man – I will rip your heart out and feed it to the bats.'

Waldobert stood in front of Claude breathing hard and swaying on his feet, sweat beginning to pour down his face. Claude could clearly see that he was almost at the point of collapse but then he quickly grabbed at a small phial which had been stored down the front of the heavy gown he was wearing.

Claude watched in a daze thinking how ridiculous Waldobert looked in the gown as he drank down the magical elixir in a flash. Immediately the effect of the drug began to explode in his body; his body went into convulsions and images of Gilroy, Dargo, his own face and Drasilla flashed across his face; it was as if his whole body was rebelling against the constant changes and was beginning to malfunction like a movie in quick motion.

His body began to spin around and around until finally he slumped for a few seconds on the ground before rearing back up again like a frenzied giant jack-in-the-box.

'I'm going to crush you into tiny pieces and stomp on you, you miniscule insignificant worm,' he growled. Steam seemed to be coming out of his ears and nostrils and his eyes were blazing in his now huge bloated grisly face like two fireballs.

I wish he would stop doing that – he is making me feel giddy, Claude thought as he stood watching him.

Waldobert suddenly roared and lunged at Claude with such ferocity that Claude was taken completely by surprise; he had been distracted and mesmerized by the images of faces flashing before his eye.

The impact of Waldobert's sudden attack threw him backwards and he stared into Waldobert's bloodshot eyes as they grappled together on the ground – all the while Waldobert's hot bubbling saliva dripped down onto Claude's face burning him on impact.

Claude screamed in agony and fury as he struggled to free himself from Waldobert's grasp.

Waldobert began to hurl more insults as he clamped his thick hands tightly around Claude's neck. Claude choked and spluttered as he began to see black spots twirling before his eyes; he could hear Waldobert's malicious laughter echoing around him and throughout the dark eerie passageway. He knew that he was not strong enough to pull away from the huge strong hands and his body went limp from the pain as Waldobert began hitting him with repeated blows, pummelling away at him; he felt the fists slamming into his throat and face until he finally fainted.

He regained consciousness almost immediately when he felt himself being dragged along the cold marble flooring. His head dropped onto his chest as blackness seemed to engulf his senses again. He forced his swollen eyes open as he was hauled into one of the torture chambers, craning his aching neck as he was dragged forward and tossed into a corner like a bag of bones; he watched as a heavy chain was being wrapped loosely around his neck. He lay there horrified as he could see bones of human remains scattered around him.

Waldobert stood looming over him smiling triumphantly at his victory over him. 'I am the mighty warrior and I will conquer you all,' he roared.

Claude struggled to his feet choking and coughing as the chain tightened around his neck. Waldobert immediately kicked out at him sending him sprawling on his back again.

'I told you, you will never conquer me – I am invincible so you had better just give up and lay there quietly or I will be forced to finish you off right here and now.'

'You are a monster and only happy when you watch people suffering,' Claude said quietly as he watched Waldobert's eyelids beginning to flutter as if he was going to fall asleep any minute as he stood before him.

'I am not in the least bit interested in your opinion of me, you mere slug of a being,' he said, his voice beginning to slur. 'You are nuffin to me, do you hear me, I will crrussh you right now until you are just sssllime seeping all over the floor and then I will skate on you.'

His eyes began to visibly roll in his head and his legs started to wobble under him as he tottered closer now until Claude could feel his hot breath burning him again and he quickly averted his face.

Waldobert suddenly stumbled almost on top of Claude but grabbing hold of the iron chain to steady himself, then reared up again still holding onto the chain and then went crashing backwards pulling the chair away from Claude's neck.

Claude seized the moment and leapt to his feet; he peered around the dark dungeon looking for a weapon and ran over to pick up an iron sledge hammer which had been tossed in the corner of the dungeon nearby some bones. He turned quickly as Waldobert began to groan; his body quivering as he lay on the cold flooring.

Claude walked stealthily over until he was standing over him and raised the mallet high above his own head before descending it swiftly down upon Waldobert's head rendering him completely senseless and crushed as he lay slumped flat out on the stone ground moaning loudly.

Although Claude was immensely surprised at how easy it had been to triumph over Waldobert, he realized that it had been due to Waldobert's progressively weakened state and he guessed that within a short space of time, he would have been weak to the point of not being able to defend himself at all but there had been no time to lose in the circumstances.

He stood looking down at the now completely warped image of Drasilla slumped at his feet groaning and slowly the image began to fade before his eyes as the gruesome image of Waldobert reappeared.

He hurriedly wrapped the heavy chain around and around Waldobert's huge bloated body until he was unable to move, making sure that the chain was locked tightly around his neck; not even Waldobert would be able to escape the heavy chain bondage tightly encasing his body. He locked the dungeon securely and peered through the iron bars as Waldobert lay there still groaning.

'You won't get away with this, I will get out of here and when I do I will come after you,' Waldobert mumbled as he slowly began to regain his senses.

Claude sank to his knees in complete exhaustion; his eyes and lip were so swollen that he could hardly see and speak. His whole body seemed to be caked in bloodied dust and cobwebs. He scrambled back up on his feet, brushed himself down and slowly ambled along the dark passageway and up the steps. He did not falter as he climbed the steep stone stairway. He could still hear Waldobert groaning loudly and calling out to him now.

He felt immensely proud of his victory over Waldobert and he couldn't wait to get back to Gilroy and together they would lead the others out of this place.

He just hoped that his somewhat bloodied appearance would not frighten them or mislead them into thinking that it was another one of Waldobert's masked trickery. But that was all over now and they could all relax when he could tell them that Waldobert was locked away helpless once and for all.

As he finally reached the last step of the never ending stairway, he could hear several voices and a dog barking; he suddenly felt a surge of renewed strength as he ran towards the sound of the voices until he could see Wally through his blurred vision bounding toward him with Errol right behind him.

Wally leapt into Claude's arms frantically slurping all over his face; tears streamed down Claude's face as he hugged Walter tightly.

'Am I ever so glad to see you my good and faithful friend,' Claude said laughing and wincing as his lips began to crack.

'Are you OK Claude,' he heard Errol say as he toppled backwards with Wally on top of him.

'Never felt better!' he replied still wincing as his cracked lip began to sting ferociously.

Chapter Thirty-Seven

Gilroy was suddenly roused by a loud joyful cry followed by deafening shrill sounds of several noisy voices hooting and hollering from above him. He stirred and stood up from the cold marble flooring where he had been laid out, still reeling from the blow to his head sustained earlier, rubbing his eyes in sheer amazement when he looked up at the stone steps where the figure of Drasilla stood calm and unruffled smiling broadly alongside Claude and Bogey. He was so engrossed and enraptured at this vision of loveliness, that he scarcely noticed the entrance of the others who now raced down the stairway and began dancing and twittering around him in their sheer excitement.

He hesitated scratching his head; *now is this really Drasilla or is it a reproduction again,* he thought as he then tentatively stepped backwards.

'Don't worry Gilroy, it really is me,' she called down smiling.

'I just want to be sure – let me have a look at your legs – lift up your skirt,' he yelled back shuffling his feet in his embarrassment.

'I will certainly not lift my skirt up,' she replied.

'How do I know that you have not got hairy legs?'

'I can assure you Gilroy that I do not have hairy legs and I thank you not to mention that again,' she said.

As Drasilla started to walk down the stone staircase, he rushed forward to the foot of the stairway with his arms extended out ready to embrace her.

'Don't you dare hug me Gilroy – don't even think about it,' she said, laughing with tears in her eyes.

'But Madam, I insist,' Gilroy sobbed as he threw his arms around her neck, planting wet slobbery kisses on her cheeks and then lifting her up and swinging her around in his utter joy.

She shuddered, grimacing as she wiped the gooey wetness from her face. She was never so happy to see all the familiar weird and wonderful faces surrounding her.

'Now please put me down my good man, I insist.'

'Oh, I'm a good man now am I?' Gilroy said laughing. 'Thank the Lord you are still in one piece; I am so happy to see you,' he continued as he now returned her back on her feet reeling from dizziness and stood back looking at her.

'And may I say after your most trying and unfortunate ordeal, you are looking as elegant and glamorous as ever and of course we would expect nothing less from you whatever situation you find yourself in.'

'Yes, well, we girls have to keep up appearances. At least we were well taken care of in the circumstances and I had all my best gowns and jewellery expressly delivered courtesy of Waldobert parading himself as Dargo.'

'A-hem, a-hem,' he now heard a voice interrupting them. 'Can we also have a little bit of attention here – we can't allow you to bathe in all the glory as usual?'

Gilroy turned and rushed to Bogey nearly knocking him over in his eagerness to hug him, planting huge slobbering kisses all over his face.

'Oh yuk, steady on,' Bogey spluttered. 'And, what is that unholy stink wafting around,' he continued now smiling. He was deliriously happy to see Gilroy and at this moment, he didn't care how bad he smelt.

'Oh my dear boy where have you been; I have been that worried about you and I have had all sorts of visions that you were imprisoned somewhere and left to die in the most squalid of conditions. Have you been eating sensibly – I hope you have been keeping to your diet; you know you have to watch your weight,' Gilroy said hardly pausing for breath, gently scolding and shaking him with affection.

'Can we skip all the nonsense here,' Claude said sighing, his eyes rolling in exasperation.

'Not me!' Bogey replied putting his arm around Claude's shoulders. 'I've been busy with Claude here plotting for your escape. Between us we have been able to rescue Claudette and Drasilla and capture Waldobert in the process and hand him over to the proper authority. And, yes you can be sure I've kept to a diet; I've hardly even eaten for the last couple of days worrying about you here.'

'You did all that without my help,' said Gilroy mockingly.

'I certainly did but we have to give most of the credit to Claude here because without him we could not have done any of it.'

'Oh don't exaggerate so Bogey,' Claude said appearing slightly embarrassed by such praise that he wasn't accustomed to.

'Yes, well Madam I think a little raise in his salary would not go amiss now,' Gilroy said directing his eyes at Drasilla and winking slyly at her.

'Gilroy will you stop that. I'm quite happy with my salary, I can tell you that Madam,' Claude said contritely, his face reddening in embarrassment. 'I don't expect any special treatment after this,' he added.

'And you certainly won't get any,' Drasilla replied but smiling and winking at Gilroy now.

'No, but I will want a raise in salary and special treatment after this,' Bogey said.

'Shuddup will ya,' Gilroy said gently slapping him around the back of his head affectionately.

'Don't forget us,' chimed in the Pug brothers holding tightly on to a lead attached to Wally looking decidedly proud of themselves.

Wally suddenly broke away and bounded over to Gilroy barking excitedly, his tongue hanging out dripping saliva and his tail wagging furiously. He stood up on his hind legs and began franticly licking Gilroy's hands.

'And, it's good to see you too boy – I can tell you that!' Gilroy said as he knelt down to nuzzle his head against Wally's. 'And, of course we could not forget all your help,' he added looking over towards the Pug brothers standing by looking proud of themselves.

'Yes, they helped a great deal,' Errol said suddenly stepping forward out of the shadow of the doorway at the top of the stairway. 'They came looking for me and guided me back to the castle although I can see now that between the two of you, you had it all under control,' he continued looking at Bogey and Claude.

'But where is Claudette?' Gilroy asked looking around.

'She wanted to go in the ambulance with Dargo, she wouldn't leave his side. He is in a pitiful condition and although I think we rescued him with not a moment to lose, I'm sure he will pull through and will completely recover, good as new, especially as Dargo has now got something to live for, if I am not mistaken. I think Claudette is completely smitten with him,' he added winking.

They all suddenly turned towards the stone stairway as an angry roar was heard along the adjoining passageway above. The Pug brothers predictably rushed towards Gilroy and clung to his legs, their small bodies visibly shaking.

'What now?' Errol said looking around at the others. 'He cannot possibly have recovered from the blow to his head. Such a blow rendered him completely senseless and I cuffed his hands and ankles.'

'Stand back,' Gilroy commanded as he shook the Pug brothers away from his legs. He quickly picked up his ball on a chain and slowly crept towards the stone stairway swinging the ball precariously around his head causing them all to back away as far from him as they could, fearful for their own safety.

'For God's sake Gilroy be careful with that great iron ball, you could do some damage to yourself,' Errol barked loudly, looking extremely anxious for the safety of the others standing around.

Gilroy dropped the ball in shock as the roar began to get louder and closer. Drasilla rushed to his side and pulled him back.

'Please be careful Gilroy! We can't be sure how much he has regained his strength and if he has fully recovered he will have ripped the handcuffs away with his teeth.'

They all gasped as Gruntle appeared at the top of the stairway roaring like a lion.

'Oh my God Gruntle, you gave us all such a fright,' Drasilla cried out hardly able to contain herself visibly shaking from head to foot.

'YOU FOOLS! I am not Gruntle, I am the mighty Waldobert. Did you think you could all escape from me that easy? I have the power to transform myself into any one of you,' he roared at them.

They all turned to look around from one face to another looking puzzled and suspicious of each other, sheer horror showing in each face.

Gruntle then began descending down the stairs laughing out loud.

'I'm just kidding, it's only me. I thought I would just play a little trick on you all,' he said laughing. He stopped midway as they all rushed up the stairway towards him menacingly; he spun round and began to quickly climb the steps but not before Errol caught up with him and grabbed him by the scruff of his neck.

'Don't you ever do that again you demented old fool,' he growled at him. 'You nearly gave us all a heart attack with your little trick. It's completely out of character and at your age you should know better.'

'Oh come on, we've all lived a nightmare for the past few days and a little bit of light entertainment at the end of it can't be all that bad,' replied Gruntle as he rubbed his grisly beard shuddering as tiny black critters began to spring out from the thick ginger growth.

'That was not in the least funny,' Bogey grunted and then in turn began howling like a demented wolf and ambled towards them.

'Now you will be the first to be tortured to death. I need to feast on your flesh now and my hunger is intense for your fresh blood,' he continued as he swaggered and lurched towards Gruntle with his arms outstretched like a sinister ghoul.

He burst into laughter and then lost his balance as Gilroy rushed at him swiping him quickly and firmly around the back of his neck.

'You idiot, can't you see that you are frightening the life out of Drasilla and not to mention the Pug brothers who have literally collapsed in a heap of quivering jelly.'

'I simply cannot believe that you would all behave like morons in such a situation – it's unbelievable and I have lost all patience now,' Drasilla said as she marched off in a huff in front of them all and up the stone stairway, her now grubby gown rustling as she moved.

'I don't know about the rest of you but I am ready to get out of here and the sooner, the better,' she continued. I can't wait to get out of this gown, have a steaming hot shower and sit down to a good breakfast. And, if you can all keep up with me, you are all invited back to my place for hot coffee and all that you can eat.'

Both Gilroy and Bogey rushed forward right behind her elbowing each other out of the way.

'That sounds good to me and I could just kill for a pint of Ginger Beer,' Gilroy said laughing. 'I think I've lost some weight since I've been here,' he then patted his shrinking stomach with pride.

'Right, enough of all this nonsense – please let's get out of here before we all turn into Waldobert,' Errol announced gruffly as he bounded up the stairway after Drasilla.

Wally who had sat obediently by the side of Errol now rushed after them all howling.

'Don't you start,' Gilroy said laughing, 'we've all heard enough howling to last us a life time.'

Epilogue

Following their escape to safety Gilroy and Bogey thereafter returned to their previous idyllic existence living their days out happily and contented in the cave with Drasilla and the fairy vampires. The tiny captured blue fairies had all been released from their glass cages and set free to return to the woods where they all buzzed around creating a wonderful array of colour and ambience.

It was rumoured that a tiny little reproduction of Gilroy was seen running around the caves much to the displeasure of Drasilla in spite of her previous warnings to him not to bother her girls, and as much as she tried to deny it to herself, he was actually quite cute. Gilroy had named him Rooney and thought he had great potential as a future burping champion and together they practised every single day.

Gilroy was very proud of his little son who bore an indistinguishable resemblance to himself and even showed promise of being just as flatulent; they were like two peas in a pod and did everything together.

Gilroy had also struck up a firm bond and friendship with Gruntle after their fateful and involuntary adventure together. Gruntle had over a short period of time thereafter carefully and conscientiously prepared a strong potion and miracle cream for Gilroy's spotty complexion. It had been an enormous relief for Gilroy to suddenly find himself cured of all the postural lumps and bumps on his face and body. He felt like a new man; a king of a man – refined and handsome beyond his wildest dreams. But as much as Gruntle tried and tried to develop a magical potion to cure Gilroy of his flatulence, alas it was an impossible undertaking thus far.

Dargo had sustained multiple injuries during his incarceration in the pit of Waldobert's dungeons but with the gentle nursing from Claudette, he slowly recovered and soon after married Claudette, whose hair regained its former glossy radiant colour. On the insistence of Drasilla, they celebrated their nuptial joining in her expansive and glittering ballroom which included magnificent burlesque performances and pole dancing routines of the highest class.

Every single element and manoeuvre in the routines had been meticulously planned and thoroughly rehearsed beforehand by Gerard, from the music to the costume requirements and his style, consistency and ability to surprise all guests with an entertaining and unique show as usual surpassed his excellence and superior abilities. The Pug brothers also gave a spectacular dance performance in their high heels – it was a dream come true for Clancy.

Clancy, Cedric and Cecil, were also awarded special honours for their bravery in helping to apprehend the Troll Warrior and were welcomed back into Drasilla's caves as Class I Security Aids, although Clancy spent most of his time in the dance studio drooling over Gerard and he was determined to become a dancer just like him.

Wally, the scruffy great Irish wolfhound, was also awarded a special honour of bravery award making Mason very proud indeed.

Claude and Baldric had become reconciled thereafter and were both happy and contented working in Drasilla's cave as her two personal and most loyal man servants.

Errol, now semi-retired from his duties as the Sheriff, concentrated on assisting his wife with her business which was also fast becoming a thriving fashion empire. With his expert advice on everything from accounting to management, finance to sales and marketing, Errol proved to be a huge asset to her prosperous business and one which Drasilla gladly contributed to with her regular orders of the fashionable costumes and gowns. And, much to Errol's discomfort, surprisingly Drasilla and Labelle became the best of friends.

Drasilla of course was happy with her life and although Gilroy continued to believe that she was saving herself for him, she kept him well at bay apart from the odd dinner and outing together and Gilroy never failed to amuse her. She always believed in time that a good man would turn up for her but she was not holding her breath.

Gilroy was certainly not an evil Troll as everybody had been led to believe; he was a good and kind person, but although he had been vindicated of all evil deeds he was never sure of being able to entirely shake off the bad reputation that he had been cursed with by his evil twin, the Troll Warrior.

Waldobert was relocated and incarcerated in a cell thereafter in the Troll kingdom; his health had gradually deteriorated until he was no longer able to walk. His dastardly crimes were heinous; he had slain young innocent fairies to live on a diet of their innocent young flesh which he believed renovated and strengthened his body and soul and the juices of which he developed in his laboratory to produce his magic elixir. So wicked was his soul that unbeknown to himself, the goodness in the elixir worked the opposite in his system, slowly rendering him without physical strength of mind and body until he became nothing more than a twisted and demented old Troll constantly babbling, making unintelligible guttural sounds, uttering profanities and constantly dribbling in the process. The mighty Troll Warrior had fallen, never to return although he could often be heard to cry out in the darkness of his dungeon 'I'll will return.'

The End